THE EXERCISE OF INTERFERING

THE SIDEKICK'S SURVIVAL GUIDE MYSTERIES, BOOK 3

CHRISTY BARRITT

COMPLETE BOOK LIST

Squeaky Clean Mysteries:

   #1 Hazardous Duty

   #2 Suspicious Minds

   #2.5 It Came Upon a Midnight Crime (novella)

   #3 Organized Grime

   #4 Dirty Deeds

   #5 The Scum of All Fears

   #6 To Love, Honor and Perish

   #7 Mucky Streak

   #8 Foul Play

   #9 Broom & Gloom

   #10 Dust and Obey

   #11 Thrill Squeaker

   #11.5 Swept Away (novella)

   #12 Cunning Attractions

#13 Cold Case: Clean Getaway

#14 Cold Case: Clean Sweep

#15 Cold Case: Clean Break

#16 Cleans to an End (coming soon)

While You Were Sweeping, A Riley Thomas Spinoff

The Sierra Files:

#1 Pounced

#2 Hunted

#3 Pranced

#4 Rattled

The Gabby St. Claire Diaries (a Tween Mystery series):

The Curtain Call Caper

The Disappearing Dog Dilemma

The Bungled Bike Burglaries

The Worst Detective Ever

#1 Ready to Fumble

#2 Reign of Error

#3 Safety in Blunders

#4 Join the Flub

#5 Blooper Freak

#6 Flaw Abiding Citizen

#7 Gaffe Out Loud

#8 Joke and Dagger

#9 Wreck the Halls

#10 Glitch and Famous (coming soon)

Raven Remington

Relentless 1

Relentless 2 (coming soon)

Holly Anna Paladin Mysteries:

#1 Random Acts of Murder

#2 Random Acts of Deceit

#2.5 Random Acts of Scrooge

#3 Random Acts of Malice

#4 Random Acts of Greed

#5 Random Acts of Fraud

#6 Random Acts of Outrage

#7 Random Acts of Iniquity

Lantern Beach Mysteries

#1 Hidden Currents

#2 Flood Watch

#3 Storm Surge

#4 Dangerous Waters

#5 Perilous Riptide

#6 Deadly Undertow

Lantern Beach Romantic Suspense

Tides of Deception

Shadow of Intrigue

Storm of Doubt

Winds of Danger

Rains of Remorse

Lantern Beach P.D.

On the Lookout

Attempt to Locate

First Degree Murder

Dead on Arrival

Plan of Action

Lantern Beach Escape

Afterglow (a novelette)

Lantern Beach Blackout

Dark Water

Safe Harbor

Ripple Effect

Rising Tide

Crime á la Mode

Deadman's Float

Milkshake Up

Bomb Pop Threat (coming soon)

Banana Split Personalities (coming soon)

The Sidekick's Survival Guide

The Art of Eavesdropping

The Perks of Meddling

The Exercise of Interfering

The Practice of Prying (coming soon)

Carolina Moon Series

Home Before Dark

Gone By Dark

Wait Until Dark

Light the Dark

Taken By Dark

Suburban Sleuth Mysteries:

Death of the Couch Potato's Wife

Fog Lake Suspense:

Edge of Peril

Margin of Error

Brink of Danger

Line of Duty

Cape Thomas Series:

Dubiosity

Disillusioned

Distorted

Standalone Romantic Mystery:

The Good Girl

Suspense:
Imperfect
The Wrecking

Sweet Christmas Novella:
Home to Chestnut Grove

Standalone Romantic-Suspense:
Keeping Guard
The Last Target
Race Against Time
Ricochet
Key Witness
Lifeline
High-Stakes Holiday Reunion
Desperate Measures
Hidden Agenda
Mountain Hideaway
Dark Harbor
Shadow of Suspicion
The Baby Assignment
The Cradle Conspiracy
Trained to Defend

Nonfiction:

Characters in the Kitchen

Changed: True Stories of Finding God through Christian Music (out of print)

The Novel in Me: The Beginner's Guide to Writing and Publishing a Novel (out of print)

CHAPTER ONE

"I DON'T WANT to do this." I fanned my face as I felt the heat rising up my neck. Fight or flight was kicking in—and I was seriously considering flight.

Michael Straley, my coworker, punched my arm, which I'd recently learned was a show of comradery and not the beginning of a fight.

"It's going to be fine, Elliot," he murmured. "True fact."

I felt anything but fine—*that* was the true fact of the matter. I might as well be part of a herd of cattle about to go in for slaughter. I could smell imminent death in the air.

There were probably thirty of us backstage. Some people paced. Others did vocal warmups—though I had no idea why since no one was actually singing for this competition. One man shook out his arms like he might throw some shoulder punches himself.

In the distance—onstage—I could hear music. Applause. An audience who might throw poop at us if we did poorly.

No, those were the monkeys that did that.

But still.

"I'd much rather be going undercover." I focused my attention back on Michael, who stood in front of me like a paramedic monitoring someone at risk for a heart attack. "I'd even rather do hours of surveillance without a bathroom in sight. Are you sure this was in my contract when I signed on with Driscoll and Associates?"

Michael frowned, almost apologetically. "Actually, it was. Velma had our lawyers add that clause in a couple years ago."

I found that hard to believe, especially given my obsession with details. "But I'm the kind of girl who reads all the fine print. I don't remember anything about this."

"It was there. It was just in the *fine* fine print. And the wording may have been a little off, but it said something about *any other duties as Oscar Driscoll sees fit.*"

I crossed my arms, my anxiety turning into irritation. "I would have never thought that lip-synching would be one of those things. Was there some kind of clause adding, 'within reason'?"

This public display of humiliation was most certainly *not* within reason.

"Driscoll and Associates enters this competition every

year." Michael leaned against the wall, a hand resting in his jeans pocket.

He removed his cowboy hat and ran a hand through his dark hair. It was so strange not seeing him in his trademark backward baseball cap. But we'd all had to dress the part for our performance. Baseball hats were out, and cowboy hats were in.

"Whoever wins gets a trophy," Michael continued. "It's a very coveted award here in Storm River."

I scooted back as one of my competitors practiced a dance move and bumped into me.

I offered a tight smile to accept his apology before turning back to Michael. "Well, that's just ridiculous. Of all the things you could receive an award for, it's really a lip-synching battle that Oscar is going to bat for?"

Why couldn't my boss focus his attention on a "good citizen" award? I could even justify some kind of Sherlock Holmes-style recognition. But lip-synching? No.

"Wait, you just used a baseball analogy." Pride warmed Michael's gaze. "I'm teaching you well."

"One day, I'll begin to understand all of these American-isms. Maybe." I'd only lived in this country for four months, and some of the culture and slang still perplexed me.

"You're going to be fine." Michael's voice turned serious, all his kidding gone as he locked gazes with me.

"I am not an onstage type of person," I reminded him,

another wave of heat climbing up my neck. "I'm the kind who likes to be behind the scenes."

My mouth needs to have moves, as the music grooves. But I think I might hurl, as I give it a whirl. I'm just not a spotlight kind of girl.

When I got nervous, I started to rhyme. It was a coping mechanism my dad had taught me.

Before I could say anything else, Oscar Driscoll himself stepped into the waiting area where we'd all gathered until it was our turn onstage. He was dressed in cowboy boots, jeans, and a white button-up shirt. It wasn't the normal look for my soap-opera-loving, lazy, good-for-nothing boss. I'd heard someone refer to him as Boss Hogg, but I wasn't sure what that meant.

The staff of Driscoll and Associates had gathered at the Oleander Resort.

This was the first time I'd ever been to Oleander, and I had to admit that I didn't like being here. I felt sick to my stomach just stepping onto the grounds.

My father had worked at this resort. It was also where he'd died of a supposed heart attack. Recently, new evidence had come to light that made me question whether his death was natural at all.

We were here with nine other teams from all around town for the thirteenth Annual Storm River Lip-Synching Competition. Everyone else around me seemed halfway excited.

Me? Not so much. It had been all I could do to get through our practices together without feeling like a fool.

Somehow, I'd found myself dressed in skinny jeans, cowboy boots, and a black leather jacket. I'd also had to don some sunglasses and learn how to strut across the stage like a supermodel.

This was a disaster in the making.

I fought the heat climbing up my neck again as I pondered what was about to happen.

Maybe it wasn't too late for me to get fired. After all, I'd only worked for Oscar for a few weeks, and I'd already been fired from this job twice.

Too bad that never worked out in my favor.

Michael leaned closer again, his own leather jacket barely concealing his black T-shirt that read "Humpty Dumpty Was Pushed."

The man loved conspiracy theories. I still wasn't sure if he was joking when he wore those T-shirts and trying to mess with people's heads, or if he really believed they were true.

Michael liked to keep parts of his life a mystery, I supposed.

"Driscoll and Associates! You guys are up next." A high-strung man wearing a headset and carrying an electronic tablet stepped backstage.

I mentally rehearsed all the moves we'd been practicing. Oscar had just sprung this on me last week, which really wasn't nearly enough time to get something like this together.

If you asked my opinion.

Which, clearly, no one had.

"Okay, Driscoll and Associates . . . I need you in the wings," Headset Man said. "You'll be going on in four minutes and thirty-two seconds."

The nauseous feeling in my stomach turned into a slight tremor that raced through my muscles. It was ridiculous, really, but I did *not* want to do this.

Michael's hands went to my shoulders, and he gently worked out the knots there. "Don't pass out on us, Elliot."

"Then don't make me do this," I said.

"We've gotten second place the past two years." Oscar rubbed his mustache, forcing the dark hairs to lay flat. "We can't let the crew at The Burger Joint beat us again this year."

I couldn't really care less about winning, but I listened to him anyway, just to be polite.

As we were ushered into the wings of the stage area, I tried to focus on my breathing.

The nine other businesses competing included the reigning champion burger joint, a car dealership, a plastic surgery practice, a construction company, a trendy boutique, a car wash, a local resort, a travel agency, and some lawyers.

I'd thoroughly enjoyed seeing the numbers being performed so far. The lawyers had done "Call Me Maybe." The car dealership—all men—were doing "Single

Ladies." The boutique employees lip-synched, "Girls Just Want to Have Fun." The golf club, "We Are the Champions."

Driscoll and Associates? "Achy Breaky Heart." Oscar said it was in honor of the cheating spouses we'd helped nail through our investigations.

I closed my eyes and mentally visualized myself walking to the right side of Oscar, just three steps behind him. I pictured myself raising my left arm and then my right. I tried to remember all the words that I needed to move my mouth to.

This whole thing seemed ridiculous. Why did people think this was fun? Next thing I knew, they'd make me do karaoke. I shuddered in horror at the thought.

"Two minutes!" Headset Man yelled.

Great. I wasn't going to get out of this, was I?

We scooted closer to the stage and, in the distance, I heard the strands of some other song playing. I really wanted to get a glimpse of what was happening out there. The plastic surgery practice was onstage, and they were doing a song called "Barbie Girl."

Americans had some interesting songs. Then again, back in Yerba, our number one hit song for an entire year had been "The Night the Clown Monkeys Came and Danced the Jig."

If I strained my neck, I could barely see the group performing.

My eyes widened when I saw one of the girls tumble on the stage. One of her coworkers quickly helped her back up.

That was going to be me, wasn't it? I was destined to make a fool of myself.

I'll look like such a fool. Not that I was ever cool. But making me do this was just plain cruel.

Just as the group came off the stage, the emcee strode across the platform and picked up the mic.

He was about to announce us.

Another flutter of nerves rushed through me.

Just as he said, "And now we would like to welcome . . . Driscoll and Associates," a scream sliced through the air.

My team members and I glanced at each other.

This was not a part of the act.

Suddenly, I forgot about the competition at hand. Michael and I ran from the wings toward the backstage area.

A crowd had already gathered near an emergency exit door. Michael and I pushed our way through them until we saw what had captured their attention.

A suit-clad man lay on the floor. Unmoving. Lifeless. Blood pooled from a wound on his abdomen.

I sucked in a breath.

Someone had killed him, I realized.

As everything blurred around me, Michael's arm slipped around my waist.

Just in time.

My knees lost their strength, and I nearly collapsed.

FIFTEEN MINUTES LATER, Michael had gotten me a cup of coffee, and I stood against the wall of the performance hall sipping on the bland, acidic drink. Right now, I almost didn't care how bad it tasted—almost being the key word.

Everyone in the competition had been sequestered here at the resort while the police investigated the scene. Until authorities knew what happened, we were all either potential suspects or witnesses and needed to give our statements.

Realistically, the plastic surgery practice could be ruled out. They'd been onstage when the crime happened. So could the men from the construction company because they'd been in the wings with us.

But that still left three other teams. The four that had already performed—the lawyers, the boutique, the car dealership, and the resort—were seated in the audience.

I listened to the chitter-chatter around me as I waited.

Especially when Headset Man wandered into the room and began to talk to one of the stagehands.

"Did you recognize that man?" Headset Guy asked, leaning close to the college-aged boy.

"I've never seen him before. I have no idea what team he was with."

"Have you talked to anybody else? Did they recognize him?"

"I've been asking around," the stagehand said. "Nobody's claiming he's with their group."

My curiosity grew. I glanced over at Michael and knew he was also listening, only not as obvious. Unlike me, Michael casually sipped his coffee and stared off into the distance. But I knew him well enough to know he was eavesdropping.

Headset Man glanced around. I quickly looked away, remembering everything I'd been taught about being a PI, including the advice to blend in.

I wasn't doing a good job of that right now as I stared at the two men while they conversed.

"Did the police say anything to you yet?" Headset Man whispered to the stagehand.

"They're just asking questions right now. This doesn't look good, though. Everyone in Storm River is going to be talking about this."

I liked to refer to this area as a playground for all things rich and fancy. For such a small town, it had five different resorts, six golf courses, and three country clubs. The rich in the area like to flaunt their money.

I didn't know much about sports here in America, but I knew that people went crazy for their teams. These resorts were much like that. When people moved into town, they got to pick their team—I mean, resort. Whatever one you picked, that's whose side you were on after that. Your lines were drawn.

It was the strangest thing I had ever seen, almost like rival groups of monkeys in the jungle waging a war on each other and marking territory by peeing at those drawn lines. Only here, it wasn't peeing. It was throwing money down the toilet.

I continued to watch everything around me. To observe how people had gathered into clusters, where they whispered nervously. I hoped to hear a theory about what had happened. Someone had to have seen something . . . right?

Meanwhile, Oscar schmoozed and acted like a politician in the making as he handed out business cards. Our administrative assistant, Velma, last time I had seen her, was sneaking some treats from the courtesy food table into her purse. That was cheapskate Velma for you.

My eyes widened when a familiar figure stepped into the room.

Detective Dylan Hunter. He could pass as Captain America's doppelganger, with his chiseled features, light-brown hair, and reserved demeanor. All he needed was a fancy shield and a mortal enemy, and he'd be all set.

He glanced around the room before his gaze stopped on me. I wasn't sure if Hunter's shoulders slumped with disappointment or if his eyes lit with a touch of pleasure. Either way, he strode through the chattering crowd toward me.

He nodded at Michael before turning to address me. "Elliot. I didn't know you were here."

The two of us weren't exactly friends, so I had no reason to tell Hunter I was participating in the competition. We didn't have that kind of relationship.

I'd first met the man while on an undercover assignment cleaning the police station. I'd also helped to solve another local case not long ago. But the two of us were far from being friends.

"Apparently, Oscar enters this competition every year." I took a sip of my coffee and nearly gagged. Now it was tasteless, acidic, *and* cold.

Hunter's gaze darkened at the mention of Oscar. There was some kind of history between them. Neither one had told me what it was yet.

"You're observant, Elliot," Hunter said. "Did you see anything while you were backstage?"

I shook my head, wishing I had something to offer him. "I have to admit, I was so nervous about competing that my skills of observation may have been a little lacking. I was distracted by visions of myself actually breaking a leg."

Hunter turned his gaze on Michael. "You?"

"I've never seen that man before. We were backstage, just about to go on, when we heard the scream."

Hunter nodded, taking notes. "I still need the two of you to stick around. It's going to take some time to go through all our witnesses here, and we may have more questions."

At least he'd said *witnesses* instead of *suspects*.

Just then, one of Hunter's colleagues walked over and nudged him. He showed Hunter a piece of paper encased in a plastic evidence bag. Hunter's eyes studied whatever was on the other side.

My curiosity spiked.

I couldn't see what was written on it, but I *really* wanted to know. I could tell by Hunter's somber expression that it was relevant.

As Hunter turned toward me, I felt myself draw back. On second thought, maybe I *didn't* want to know.

"Are you sure you didn't know this man?" Hunter studied my face, the scrutiny making me cringe like a kinkajou being spotted by an exotic pet collector.

"I'm sure," I told him. "I mean, I didn't get a good look at him. But I don't know that many people in town yet."

"What's going on?" Michael stepped closer, a knot between his eyes and an almost protective sound to his voice.

"This was found in his pocket." Hunter turned the bag around. My name was scrawled on the piece of paper, my photo printed below it.

The blood drained from my face as I realized I had some kind of connection with this man who had been murdered.

My knees began to feel weak again. But, before I sank to the ground, Michael grabbed one arm and Hunter took the other.

It looked like today was going to be a longer day for me than for the rest of the people here.

CHAPTER TWO

TEN MINUTES LATER, I sat across from Hunter in the resort manager's office. The ever-dignified Palmer Birmingham IV was letting Hunter use the space for his interrogations. I'd been introduced to the man earlier, and he screamed snooty and pretentious.

His office space was large, with four windows facing the river. The walls had been painted a nice gray color and artfully decorated with nautical scenes.

I knew that Hunter's colleagues were busy questioning everybody else who had been at the event to learn if they'd seen anything. They'd divided up and were getting everyone's name, number, and statement. It was going to take a while.

Hunter had somehow scored this office for the top

contenders. Top contender witnesses or suspects? I wasn't sure.

Only moments ago, I'd definitely been a potential witness. Now, I had a connection with the dead man. That was a game changer, as Michael might say.

"Elliot, I need for you to be direct with me." Hunter's gaze locked on mine. "Are you sure you don't recognize this man?"

My fingers rubbed against each other as they rested in my lap. "I'm sure. I've never seen him. I mean, I've never seen him until today. And only then after he was already dead."

A moment of amusement flashed in Hunter's eyes before quickly disappearing. "Are you and your colleagues at Driscoll and Associates working on any cases right now where someone might have a vendetta against you?"

I reviewed the recent investigations we'd been involved with. It didn't take long, considering I'd only worked for Oscar for a few weeks. "We've mostly been doing insurance cases over the past week or two. Nothing that seems dangerous or worthy of a murder. Pretty boring stuff, to be honest."

Hunter shifted and leaned toward me, and I knew he was about to drive home some kind of point. "Elliot, is there any other reason somebody might have your name in their pocket?"

My mind raced. There *was* one explanation I could think of. But it involved details I hadn't shared with anybody.

Not Michael.

Not my mom.

Not my sister.

No one.

I had good reason for it.

I didn't know whom I could trust. Whomever I told could become a target, so I had to be careful. The lives of the people I cared about could depend on my discernment.

The pressure nearly suffocated me.

My gaze fluttered up to Hunter's as I wondered how much I should say. If this was pertinent to the investigation then I needed to share . . . right? It would be the responsible thing.

"Elliot?" Hunter continued to stare at me, waiting for my response.

"Uh . . ." I still had no idea how much to say. Once I opened this can of caterpillars, I knew there would be no going back.

I stared at Hunter. At his handsome face. Intelligent eyes. Steadfast demeanor.

He seemed trustworthy. But was he? How could I know?

I used to trust my instincts, but I'd stopped doing that a while ago—right after the man I loved had ghosted me. Michael had told me that was the proper word to describe what Sergio had done when he'd called off our engagement via a text.

"Elliot?" Hunter repeated, scrutinizing me from across the massive desk.

I squirmed and swallowed hard, still unsure. "I, uh . . ."

"You can tell me, Elliot." His voice sounded soothing, beckoning me to trust him.

But could I? Did I really want to go there? If I said the words aloud, I'd be throwing things in motion. There would be no turning back.

"You're not going to believe me if I tell you," I started.

I'd just confessed that there was something there. It had been the first step of admission. As the words left my mouth, I expected to feel relieved.

I didn't.

Instead, I thought I might throw up. My hands went to my stomach as I felt acid stirring in my gut.

Hunter moved around to the other side of the desk and lowered himself into the chair across from me. His actions, his words, his gaze . . . they all seemed purposeful. Calming, almost. It was part of what made him a good detective. He made people want to trust him.

But that could also be dangerous.

"Try me," he said. "You might be surprised."

I drew in a deep breath. Here went nothing.

"Don't say I didn't warn you," I murmured.

I was still delaying, putting off the inevitable.

"I'll keep that in mind."

I ripped the Band-Aid off. "I found out recently that my father was actually a spy in Yerba. A month after we moved to the States, he died—while working here at the resort. A few weeks ago, I found an old journal of his that indicated his death may not have been from natural causes like authorities suspected."

I sat there and waited. I'd spilled the words quickly before I could change my mind. My story was a lot for Hunter to comprehend, so I gave him time.

Hunter didn't say anything for a few seconds before finally murmuring, "Your dad was a spy?"

I took my cowboy hat off and ran a hand through my dark hair. "That's right. I didn't know that until after he died. He always told me he had a boring job with the government. But the journal he'd hidden for me laid it all out."

It still seemed surreal to think about.

Hunter shifted, but his gaze never left me. "Is that the reason your family moved here to Storm River?"

"I suspect it was part of the reason. As you know, my sister needs better health care, and our country was about to implode. We got out just in time. But now that I know more, I also have to wonder if my father came here so easily in return for trading information or something."

Hunter's eyes narrowed, and he nodded slowly, thoughtfully, as he continued to process everything. "Did he have any contacts in this area?"

I let out a long breath, trying to think his question through. "Not that I know about. But, honestly, there's so much that I don't know about my dad. I'm just beginning to discover all of it."

Hunter leaned back, his gaze looking distant with thought as his pupils subtly flickered back and forth. "So you think that your father being a spy might be the reason why somebody would be here at the resort with your name and photo in his pocket?"

I squirmed again as the truth tried to escape from my lips like rioting prisoners from behind bars. The truth was that there was a lot of danger in releasing these thoughts I'd bottled up for so long.

"The other fact of the matter is that I've felt like I'm being watched lately."

"Being watched how?" His eyes narrowed.

"It's just a feeling, really." I shrugged. "Well, maybe it's more than that. Someone did follow me, at least once. But I don't know why somebody would be watching me and following me."

My thoughts were a jumbled mess, and speaking them out loud did nothing to change that.

"Maybe someone thinks you have something of your father's? Maybe they see you and your family as a threat? If your father was perceived as betraying his country, somebody could want revenge."

I shuddered when I heard the theory voiced aloud. "My father is already dead. Hurting us can't hurt him anymore."

My voice caught as the words left my lips. I hadn't expected to feel such a slap of grief with my statement. But the emotion had surprised me, reminding me of my loss. My heart ached, a piece of it missing.

"We're going to keep looking into this man, see if we can find out his identity and if he has any connection to Yerba," Hunter assured me.

"That's probably a good idea."

"I'll be in touch with more questions. In the meantime, you need to be careful, Elliot. I mean it."

I nodded, reaching for the chair's arms so I could push myself up and get out of here. "I will be. Thank you. Can I go now?"

"You can go."

I stood, the chair practically falling behind me as I did. I grabbed an arm and managed to steady it before it crashed onto the wood floor.

Suddenly, I couldn't wait to get home.

I felt like I was suffocating in the past. In the present.

My life had formed a picture that I'd never envisioned—or wanted.

I paused, one more question on my mind. "By the way, I guess this means the competition is off?"

Hunter glanced up from his notes and nodded. "It's done."

At least I could rejoice in that good news.

MICHAEL WAS WAITING for me outside the office when I emerged. Without skipping a beat, he took my arm and led me away from anybody who might be listening. Finally, we stopped near a bank of windows facing the river.

"What's going on?" He lowered his voice and leaned toward me, looking like nothing else around us existed except this conversation. "Are you okay?"

Was I okay? I was still processing everything. The dead man backstage seemed like something that happened in a bad dream not reality.

"I think I'm okay," I finally said.

"Elliot, why in the world would your name and picture be in that man's pocket?" Michael didn't waste any time getting right to the point. He was that kind of guy—direct and to the point.

I shook my head, entirely uncomfortable with the whole situation. I'd wanted to keep my secrets buried for as long as I could, but that was no longer possible.

I didn't know how much I should tell Michael. I already felt exhausted from rehashing everything with Hunter. What had happened was a part of my past that I didn't want exposed to people here. Not yet.

"I have no idea," I finally said.

Michael stooped lower until his eyes met mine. Certainly he knew I wasn't telling him everything. But I had no obligation to pour all the details out to my coworker.

Sure, he'd also been a friend lately. He was probably becoming one of my closest friends since I'd moved here.

But there were some things that were just best left private, things like life or death matters.

"Elliot, you know you can talk to me if you need anything." Michael's gaze still prodded mine.

His words melted something inside me. More than anything, I wanted someone I could share all my worries and concerns with. I just wasn't sure Michael was that person.

I wanted to trust him. I really did. But the more people who knew, the more people who could potentially be in danger. And Michael had a seven-year-old daughter at home to think about.

I rubbed my throat, my decision made at the thought of Chloe. "I don't know what's going on."

Michael stared at me, looking like he wanted to believe me but didn't. Instead of calling me out on my lie, he nodded slowly, as if resigning himself to backing off—for now.

"Is Hunter going to look into this?" he asked instead. "Is he going to give you some type of protection detail until he knows what's going on?"

"He didn't say that. I promised to be careful."

Michael's gaze lingered on me a moment longer, his lips twitching as if he held back on saying something. "I don't like this, Elliot."

I shivered and rubbed my arms. "I don't like it either. The good news is that Hunter said I could leave now."

"Oscar and Velma just left. They offered to stick around, but I told them I'd make sure you got home okay. I figured the more people who could clear out of here, the better. It's been a madhouse."

"People are mad?"

"No, that means . . . never mind." He shook his head.

It seemed like people said that a lot.

"At least I didn't have to go onstage," I offered finally with a sheepish grin.

"That's one way to look on the bright side." Michael took my arm and led me toward the door. "Come on, let's get out of here."

As he ushered me past the people still remaining in the lobby, I studied each of them. Two ladies sat behind the front desk. A bellhop lingered near the door. Several tourists with suitcases parked at their feet stood near a fancy couch. A few people who appeared to have been in the audience of the competition, based on the programs in their hands, looked lost and bewildered as they waited to be questioned.

Were one of those people a killer? It was doubtful.

Three teams had been backstage at the time. The burger place, the car wash, and the travel agency.

Then again, it wasn't exactly like there was security standing guard near the backstage area. None of the teams were celebrities, and people weren't exactly clamoring for our autographs.

I also remembered how nobody had claimed to recognize the victim. At least, nobody that I'd heard about. Was that man not even associated with this competition? Had he just shown up here trying to find me and somehow ended up dead?

I shivered again.

As soon as Michael and I stepped outside into the fading sunlight, my lungs loosened just a bit.

Michael kept his hand on my arm as we began walking down the sidewalk. We'd actually parked at the office and walked over. It was five blocks, but the day had been beautiful and the exercise nice.

I wasn't going to complain about walking now either. Something about the movement helped me to sort out my thoughts. The sun had almost disappeared, bringing with it a temperate breeze. Storm River, despite its shadows, really could be a lovely town.

"I can't believe that happened." Michael shoved his hands into his pockets as he glanced around the tidy downtown area.

"Me neither. I keep replaying what happened. You didn't see that man before the competition, did you?"

"I didn't. From the scuttlebutt I heard backstage, nobody else recognized him either."

"Do you know if that man . . . had a weapon on him?" The question had been begging for my attention.

Michael cast a sharp glance at me. "I didn't hear. Why?"

"He had my name and photo. Was he coming to talk to me? Or was he coming to . . . ?" *Kill me.*

I started to say the words but nearly choked on them instead.

"Maybe there's a perfectly logical explanation for all of this," Michael said. "Let's give the police some time to work."

Even though he said those words, I had a hard time believing that's what he was going to do. Michael was a great investigator. I knew he was probably itching to find out some answers for himself.

Would he include me in that quest for answers? I didn't think so. He probably thought I was too fragile right now for that.

Maybe I was. I still wasn't sure.

As we rounded the corner near a candy shop, I stopped in my tracks.

A familiar figure came into view, and my mouth dropped open.

"Elliot?" The woman's mouth also dropped open.

It was . . . my mom.

CHAPTER THREE

I TOUCHED MY THROAT, my mind racing. "Mama . . . I didn't expect to see you here. I thought you were working today."

Her gaze went to Michael before flashing back to me. "I had to run to the dentist this evening after work. Remember? I've had that toothache for two weeks now. Turns out, it was a cavity."

I vaguely recalled her saying something about that this morning. "Now that you mention it, I do remember that. I'm surprised you got an appointment so late."

"It's at the community clinic, and they have late hours on Wednesday. Most of the staff donate their time after their regular work hours." Her gaze scanned me up and down. "Why are you dressed like an urban cowgirl?"

I glanced down at my outfit. "Like this? It's a long story. A work thing."

Her gaze went to Michael, reservation still stretching across her features. "And who is this?"

"This is my . . . coworker. Michael Straley."

Michael stretched out his arm, "Ma'am."

"Michael, this is my mom, Maureen."

As the two of them shook hands, I watched my mom's face brighten. Michael and his manners were getting her approval right now. I supposed that was a good thing.

Since we'd moved here, my mom seemed to have aged ten years. She'd always looked youthful for her age, and people had even mistaken us as sisters in the past. But the circles beneath her eyes were more pronounced now. Even her light-brown hair somehow seemed limp. But it was the dull sheen to her gaze that really drove it all home.

All of this had been harder on my mom than she'd ever admit.

Today, she wore her long hair in a braid, and she'd donned a khaki skirt that came to her knees, sandals, and a striped button-up blouse.

"It's so nice to finally meet somebody from Elliot's work." My mom offered a soft smile toward Michael.

"It's nice to meet you too," Michael said. "We are all thrilled to have Elliot at the office."

At his words, my anxiety climbed even higher. I played

out various scenarios as to how this conversation was going to go.

Not well.

That was the one thing all the scenarios had in common.

I hadn't told my mom that I was working for a PI. When she assumed Driscoll and Associates was a law firm . . . I'd just let her think that.

Guilt pressed on me.

"Elliot really seems to have taken to working at the law firm," my mom continued. "She likes it so much more than that insurance company. That job never suited her."

"The law firm . . ." Michael's voice held an underlying question.

I squeezed his arm, begging him to go along with me. "That's right. Driscoll and Associates."

Something changed in his eyes, and he nodded. After a lingering glance at me, he looked back at my mom and smiled. "Oh, yes. It's a great place. I've been there five years myself."

"I'm so glad." My mom reached forward and squeezed my hand. "I'm so glad I ran into you. Maybe you can bring Michael over sometime and I'll make some of my *Aji de Gallina*."

"I don't know what that is, but I'll take it," Michael said.

"It's a creamy chicken dish, and it's delicious," Mama said. "Isn't it, Elliot?"

"It is," I agreed, anxious for this conversation to be over.

"We'll have you over to try it sometime. You'll love it. Besides, I've been anxious to get to know some of Elliot's new friends."

Michael grinned. "I look forward to it."

I didn't release the breath from my lungs until my mom disappeared out of sight.

Then I looked up at Michael, begging him for understanding before I even said a word. "I'm sorry about that."

"She thinks you work for a law firm?" he whispered, twisting his head in confusion.

"My mom is the most God-fearing woman I know. But she struggles so much with worry, especially in the past few months. I knew if I told her I was working for a private eye that she wouldn't sleep at night. That she would think this line of work was too dangerous."

"Okay . . ."

He obviously didn't understand still.

"So when she assumed that Oscar Driscoll and Associates was a law firm . . . I didn't correct her." I shook my head, disappointed with myself. "I knew I should. But then the days passed, and I realized that correcting her at that point would be even worse. So I let it go."

"Elliot . . ." Michael's head fell to the side. "You don't seem like the type to lie to your mom."

"I'm not. I'm a rule follower. Or I used to be. Lately, I don't feel like I know who I am. There have been too many changes, too quickly." I hadn't expected to be so honest. But the admission felt good. I'd been keeping so many things bottled up inside lately.

Michael squeezed my arm. "I know who you are, Elliot Ransom."

I lifted my chin, bracing myself for whatever he was about to say. "And who is that?"

A liar. A faker. A fraud.

"You're somebody who has a heart for other people. Who would do anything to help those you love. And you have a great eye for spatial intelligence that will either be your biggest help or your biggest hindrance."

I released my breath, along with a relieved chuckle.

He pretty much had nailed that part of me. I knew all those things were true. But it was the other things in my life that had me worried.

I couldn't call myself a Christian and then lie to people in order to get answers. I'd always assumed I was a list-making, file-organizing, appointment-setting administrator. But maybe there was another part of me that was more like my dad than I had ever realized.

Could I have a secret spy hidden down deep inside?

As if my personality crisis wasn't enough, the confusion concerning my love life was enough to be a case study in muddled thinking.

"I appreciate that, Michael," I finally said. "And I'm sorry I put you in the position to not be able to tell the truth."

A shadow fell over his gaze. "I don't feel good about doing

that. I especially don't feel good about doing that if your mom actually invites me over for dinner sometime."

"If she said she was going to invite you over, then she will. That's my mom."

"I'm going to have trouble not telling her the truth." His lips squeezed together.

I could tell he meant the words, and I appreciated his integrity.

"I understand," I said. "When she invites you for dinner, I'll figure out something. An excuse as to why you can't come. I don't want to put you in that position."

"I didn't say I wanted you to do that. I kind of want to see what makes Elliot Ransom Elliot Ransom. There's a lot about you that I don't know."

Something about his words caused my throat to tighten. Why did the thought of him knowing too much about me seem so terrifying right now? "There's really nothing much to see. I'm not that interesting."

His gaze locked with mine. "I beg to differ, *InvestigaDora*."

My jaw dropped open. "Does Oscar call me that?"

"Sometimes."

"He's such a loser."

"He is. But it's clever."

"I can't argue with that."

Something about the look Michael gave me made my cheeks flush. Why was I reacting this way? And to Michael, of all people?

I looked away before he could see the heat rising in me. "I guess we'll just have to cross that bridge with my mom when we get there then."

We kept walking until we reached the building housing Driscoll and Associates. Yet my thoughts were anywhere but at the office.

SINCE THE LIP-SYNCHING competition had officially been an after-work-hours activity, I had no reason to stay at the office. Part of me wanted to. I wanted to dig into this murder, to see what I could find out about this man who'd been killed.

But I knew it was useless to search now. For starters, I didn't even have the man's name. Where would I even begin to find it? Besides, Michael needed to get home to his daughter and wouldn't be able to help. Without his expertise, there was little I could do.

Instead, he walked me to my car, gave a little salute, and made me promise I would call him if I needed him. Then I climbed into my old clunker and started home.

It seemed slightly anticlimactic to head home after something like this. But I didn't know what else to do. Besides, having some time to sort out my thoughts seemed like a good idea. I didn't want to do anything rash.

It was already getting dark outside as I drove down the

road. The competition had started at 5:30, and it was nearing eight o'clock now.

I glanced into my rearview mirror and felt my back muscles tighten. Was the car in the lane behind me copying my every move?

You would think I would be an expert on things like this by now. But I wasn't.

I gripped the steering wheel of my beat-up old Buick.

I needed to figure out if this person was tailing me or not. The feeling could simply be my paranoia acting up.

Cautiously, I made a right-hand turn, heading out of town instead of into my neighborhood.

As I waited to see what the car behind me would do, I gripped the wheel even tighter.

I glanced into my rearview mirror again.

The car had also turned.

My pulse quickened.

Did this have something to do with the man who'd been found dead? I knew I might be reading too much into this, but what if that man had shown up today to kill me? Just like someone may have killed my father? Since this guy hadn't succeeded, would someone else take his place?

I realized there was a hole in my theory, however. If someone had come to kill me, why had that person ended up dead instead of me? So much still didn't make sense. I'd have to figure that out later. Right now, I needed to focus on losing this guy behind me.

I glanced at the car one more time. It was a dark sedan with tinted windows. I couldn't tell anything about the driver inside.

As I approached an intersection, I made a split-second decision. I jerked my wheel to the left.

I barely managed to dodge the oncoming traffic. Drivers laid on their horns and threw on brakes to avoid me.

"I'm so sorry," I muttered, even though I knew none of those other drivers could hear me.

As I made it onto the other street in one piece, I let out a breath. I needed to get my thoughts under control even as my heart pounded furiously.

I glanced behind me. Had I lost the guy following me?

I didn't see him.

No one dared get too close to me after that maneuver, I supposed.

Maybe I'd bought myself some time.

With my heart still rapid-fire pounding against my chest, I continued down the road. I glanced behind me one more time for good measure.

I still didn't see the car.

Maybe I'd lost the driver.

But the bigger question was—how could I lose him for good?

CHAPTER FOUR

BACK AT HOME I talked to my mother and my sister for a few minutes. My mom had gushed about meeting Michael, and I had to remind her that we were just friends.

But I heard the subtext of her words. She'd been worried about me not making friends or fitting into this new life in the United States.

Strange that I hadn't realized that until this moment. I supposed I figured that Mama had poured all of her worry into my sister, Ruth. My sister had cystic fibrosis and was getting worse all the time.

As I'd chatted with them over tea and *crema volteada*—a flan-like dessert—I'd been careful not to mention anything about what happened at the lip-synching competition tonight. Part of me thought that maybe I should, just in case my mom and sister were in danger also. But neither of them had mentioned anything about any unusual occurrences.

Most of all, I didn't want my mom to worry. I knew that's exactly what she would do if I told her. So I decided to keep it all a secret until I knew more information.

I suppose it was my way of trying to protect her, though I could see the flip side of that also. If she didn't know the danger she was in, how could she be safe?

I didn't have all the answers. I wished the right decision would light up the nighttime sky like a meteor shower.

No such luck.

After our conversation wrapped up, I slipped into my room, changed into my pajamas, and sat on my bed. I reached over to the wooden jewelry box my dad had made me with the hidden compartment at the bottom. I pulled out the journal my father left me.

I'd been reading a new entry every day, and I was about halfway through.

He hadn't started it until we moved here to America, and he had only been alive for the first thirty days. Some days, he must have written two entries.

As I leaned back against my headboard, I wondered how he'd managed to write all this without my mother catching him. The fact that my dad hadn't said anything to my mom about his life being in danger only indicated to me more that I also needed to keep it quiet for now. I would follow his example.

I ran my fingers across his familiar scrawl. Papa had always been the storyteller, the adventurous one, and the person who loved teaching me life lessons in the real world.

Through trips to the jungle. Fishing excursions. Watching nature.

Don't get me wrong. My mom was great. She was a missionary turned homemaker who loved her community and who'd often made meals for those in need. She'd taught little kids in the town about Jesus. She never minded getting dirty, and she was always there to support her family.

I admired the life that she'd lived.

But I didn't know what I wanted for my future anymore.

In Yerba, I had worked for a government legislator. I'd made sure his schedule was lined up. That he never forgot names or birthdays. I had helped to organize events in his honor and had even assisted in writing some speeches.

I'd lived on my own. I'd been engaged, and I'd made a nice life for myself.

But then everything had been turned upside down. My fiancé had broken up with me. My country had imploded. And I'd moved to the States.

I stared at my dad's journal for another moment. What should I do now? How did I find out who the dead man was? Who had killed him? Who was following me? And why were all these things happening?

I closed my eyes, wishing I could hear my father's voice. Wishing he could give me some advice on the situation.

Wishing he could tell me some of the things that had gone to the grave with him.

Did Papa come here for reasons other than what he'd shared? Why did he have a premonition that he might be killed?

I stared at his words for this entry. Mostly what he had left me with was somewhat of a survival guide. Today's entry was about what he liked to call the pothole theory.

He said if you kept your eyes on the obstacle in front of you, it would only become more of an obstacle. But if you kept your eyes on the clear path that you needed to take, that was where you would go.

It sounded like some type of Yerbian wisdom.

So was I keeping my eyes on my problems and obstacles right now? I didn't know. That very well could be the case. How did I look at the goal—figuring out what had happened to my father?

I closed the journal and held it to my chest. I needed to figure out how I was going to keep the people I loved safe. Because now that my dad was gone, I was taking it upon myself to become the guardian of my family.

But I still had a lot to learn before I could officially claim that title and before I could do so without getting myself killed. Finding answers involved interfering in matters that I was certain could lead to trouble.

I was going to need to learn how to do that while refining my survival skills.

CHAPTER FIVE

AS SOON AS I walked into work the next morning, I was summoned into Oscar's office. Michael was already seated inside, along with a pretty blonde woman I had never seen before.

"Elliot, this is Marla Burns," Oscar said. "She's our new client."

I nodded at the woman, and she nodded back, all prim and proper.

I quickly observed her. She was probably in her fifties and thin with long, blonde hair. I had a feeling she'd had plastic surgery. Something about the way her eyes turned up and her lips plumped gave me that impression.

Oscar motioned for me to sit down, so I took the chair next to Michael and waited.

"Why don't you go ahead and explain to all of us what's going on here," Oscar directed Marla.

The woman ran her manicured hand across her little black dress. "To start, I would like to say that I am a watta botta motta."

Michael and I glanced at each other.

What had she said?

Michael spoke first. "A what?"

"A watta botta motta."

"Water bottle model." The slight warning in Oscar's voice clearly indicated we shouldn't push. "You try to say it five times fast."

Marla smiled as if self-conscious and shook her head. "I know it makes me less credible that I can't say it, but it's a real tongue twister. I have never been able to string those words together." She let out a nervous laugh.

"A water bottle model, huh?" Michael repeated. "That's interesting. Never met one of those before."

She nodded. "That's right. Perhaps you saw my commercials several years back for World's Best Water?"

Michael snapped his fingers, and his eyes lit with recognition. "You were the lady in those commercials!"

I had no idea what they were talking about. So I listened instead.

Marla nodded, any of her earlier discomfort disappearing. She beamed as she said, "That's right. That was me."

She turned her head to the side, grabbed a bottle from

her purse, and demonstrated how to drink it like a rock star. I had to admit that she did form a very nice profile.

"She did for water bottles what Cindy Crawford did for Coke back in the eighties," Michael said.

"That means nothing to me," I reminded him. I'd been immune to American culture for the first twenty-six years of my life.

"It was a big deal," Michael said. "Let's just leave it at that."

Oscar cleared his throat. "Marla has been receiving some threats lately, and she would like our help getting to the bottom of it."

"What kind of threats?" I asked. Maybe I could add something meaningful to this part of the conversation instead of feeling totally clueless.

"I got dead roses, for starters." Her voice wavered, and her eyes clouded with distress. "I also got chocolates that look deformed. I threw them away and figured they were poisoned. Then I got a note that says, 'I have my eye on you.' It's all got me creeped out."

"You got these all at your home address?" Michael asked.

"That's right. It just started a couple weeks ago. So far, I've gotten one every Friday and Saturday while I'm out with my friends. On Fridays, we have spa days. And Saturdays my friends and I have a standing brunch date."

"Do you have any idea who the sender could be?" I asked.

"It's hard to say. I have a lot of admirers." She shifted and crossed one shapely leg over the other ankle. "At least, I used to back in my heyday of being a watta botta motta. Age can do horrible things to a woman's beauty."

I wanted to argue with her, but I knew this wasn't the time or the place. But I refused to give in to the notion that beauty was only for the young. Maybe that was easy for me to say now because I was only twenty-seven years old. But I truly believed that women only got more beautiful with age.

"Could you make a list of anybody who has given you any problems lately?" Michael asked.

"Of course. I'll get started on that right away."

Oscar looked at Michael and me and flipped his hand in the air, dismissing us from his presence. "I'll have Velma get all her information. You two can go for now. Marla and I are going to catch up for a minute."

Sounded like the two of them might know each other. Interesting.

At least, I had a new case to distract myself with. That was a good thing.

But as soon as I stepped from Oscar's office, I saw somebody else sitting in the waiting area near Velma.

Detective Hunter.

And it could only mean one thing.

Either he had more questions or he had an update. Either way, I was anxious to hear what he had to say.

A FEW MINUTES LATER, Hunter and I were seated in the office Michael and I shared. Michael had volunteered to sit out in the reception area with Velma while Hunter and I spoke. However, only a glass wall and door separated the areas.

Hunter sat at my desk, and I pulled an extra chair around from my desk and placed it a good three feet away from him.

Then I waited for whatever it was he was about to say.

"I have been working on the case. As far as we can ascertain, our victim was not a part of the competition, nor did anybody there acknowledge that they had invited him or that they knew him."

"Who was he then?" I asked.

"That's a great question. We've been trying to figure that out, and we haven't had any luck yet."

Disappointment bit deep. "How is that possible? I just figured with all the technology that was out there ..."

"Normally, we might find some form of ID on a victim like this. But he didn't even have any car keys with him, nor were any unclaimed vehicles in the lot. So we couldn't identify him that way."

"What about his fingerprints?" There had to be some other way, especially in this day and age. I'd felt so certain that I'd get a name today.

"We're running his prints through the system, but it's going to take at least a few days to get any results. We haven't had any hits yet."

"That's . . . unfortunate." I fought a frown, not wanting to sound ungrateful.

"We did discover that the murder weapon was a sharp pointy object that wasn't incredibly long."

"A knife?"

"Shorter than that. Thicker also. We're still looking into it."

This wasn't exactly the news I wanted to hear. I hoped Hunter had come here today with answers that would give me some clarity as to what happened.

I knew nothing more today than I'd known yesterday.

Hunter shifted, his gaze zeroing in on me. "I wanted to check in, to see if you had remembered anything. Now that you've had some time to sleep on it, to think about it . . ."

I shook my head. "I thought about it all night. I replayed everything. The man is not familiar to me."

Hunter lowered his voice and glanced out the glass wall as if to make sure no one could hear. "What about your dad? Were you able to think of anybody who might have had a vendetta against him here in the States?"

"Here in the States? No." I kept my voice soft and leaned closer. "That's not to say that somebody didn't follow us here from Yerba. Or to say that somebody in the country's new government isn't in play."

"Your dad never talked to you about stuff like that?"

"He didn't. But knowing what I do now, it wouldn't surprise me if my father discovered something about the government and tried to stop everything that happened. I know Yerba is in a world of hurt right now, especially since the new embargoes were imposed on the country. The rich still have their money, but the poor . . . they're starving."

It hurt my heart to say those words out loud. Nobody should have to go through that. If I could do something to help anybody there, I would. But I still couldn't even cross over those borders. Not if I had any hope of getting out again.

Hunter stared at me, watching my every move, my every expression. "Maybe there's a chance that somebody saw your dad as a traitor so they're coming after you as a result."

I looked through the glass and saw Michael glance at us. Of course, he was curious about what was going on in here. He offered a subtle nod before turning back to Velma and continuing his conversation with her.

I turned back to Hunter, remembering his question. "If that's true, then who killed the person who was looking for me?"

Hunter frowned. "I can tell you've thought this through."

"I have. But I haven't been able to draw any conclusions. Believe me, I've tried."

Hunter nodded. "We're going to continue to look into this man. We're checking video footage so we can try to figure out where he came from. I just thought I should check in with you."

"I appreciate that," I told him. "If I think of anything, I will let you know."

He stared at me another moment before nodding and rising to his feet. "Thanks, Elliot. I'll be in touch then."

I opened the door for him, and Hunter stepped outside. He offered brief nods to Michael and Velma before leaving.

And as soon as he was out the door, Michael and Velma turned to me, obviously waiting for an explanation.

I squirmed.

What exactly was I going to tell them?

CHAPTER SIX

I COMPOSED myself before saying anything to Michael and Velma. I brushed my hair out of my face, straightened the little black sweater I wore to keep me warm from the blaring AC, and licked my lips.

Finally, I announced, "There aren't any updates on the dead man. I know that's what you two really want to know."

Michael frowned. "I was hoping we could put this behind us."

"Me too." I sat in the chair across from him and felt my shoulders slump.

"I'm sure you're anxious to reschedule the lip-synching competition as well." Michael watched me, a sparkle in his gaze.

Of all the things I was anxious about, rescheduling the

most humiliating experience of my life wasn't at the top of my list. Michael knew that.

I did one of his shoulder punches. "You know me so well."

"Don't I, though?" He grinned before turning serious again. "So what now?"

"I'm not sure. I guess let the police figure things out. I'll wait and see and be careful in the process."

His eyes darkened. "I don't like the sound of that."

"I don't either, but what else can I do?"

"I did have an idea." Michael stood and stepped toward the door. "Come on. Let's get out of here."

I pointed back at Oscar's office. I hadn't seen Marla come out, and I assumed we still needed more details from her before we could start our investigation. "Don't we need to wait for Oscar and Marla to finish the conversation so we can start on her case?"

"I have a feeling they're going to be a while. Oscar will call us when he's ready for us to start."

I glanced at Velma, who nodded in agreement. I was going to have to trust their judgment here.

A few minutes later, Michael ushered me outside, and we headed toward the parking lot behind the building.

"So what do you know that I don't?" I asked him. There was obviously something I was missing, that I wasn't privy to concerning this new case.

"About what?"

"Oscar and Marla."

Michael's eyebrows flickered up in surprise then back down, as if the question disappointed him. "Oh. Marla was Oscar's first wife."

My eyes widened. "Really? There's so much I don't know about that man."

Michael gave me a half side-glance, half eye roll. "Believe me, you don't want to know everything."

He could very well be right about that. Oscar had become somewhat of a celebrity when he solved a big national case. He'd gotten a book deal and a TV movie out of it.

"So where are we going?" I asked as we climbed into Michael's messy minivan.

"I thought we could head back to the resort and talk to a few people there."

My breath caught as I realized what he was saying. "You're going to help me find out who this dead guy is?"

He looked at me, appearing halfway insulted that I'd ever doubted him, and then cranked his engine. "Of course. Until we know if you're safe or not, we need to get some answers."

Gratitude filled my heart. Michael was such an answer to prayer.

Then another thought hit me.

"Won't Oscar be upset? He doesn't like us taking on assignments that he hasn't explicitly given." I'd discovered that when I had done just exactly that and got fired not long ago.

Michael started down the road. "Oscar gave his stamp of approval on this. I talked to him this morning before you came in."

Michael certainly seemed to have a way with Oscar, and I wasn't sure why the two had a soft spot for each other. I didn't ask any questions. I just nodded and went along with it.

As we traveled down the road, I pointed at a mega church up ahead. Not only was the building huge, but the pastor and his wife had their faces plastered on a sign out front.

Houses of worship like that one were so different from what I'd experienced where I'd grown up. Church wasn't about celebrity. It was a place for people who weren't afraid to get their hands dirty as they dug into the gospel and tried to be the hands and feet of Jesus in real and practical ways.

"Why are you making that face?" Michael followed my gaze. "You don't like big churches?"

"I didn't say that. I'm sure they do a lot of good. They're just not my thing."

"Why not?" He sounded like he honestly wanted to know.

How much should I say? I wasn't sure, and I definitely didn't want to get into any arguments about it.

I finally told him, "When I think about all the money that's been poured into those buildings to make them look good, I start thinking about the poor and how much better served that money would be going toward helping people in those situations. I don't know. . . sometimes I think that big churches seem more like businesses than they do places of worship. That's just my opinion, of course."

"No, I understand what you're saying."

I glanced at him. "Do you go to church?"

I had a feeling Michael did, but I'd never directly asked him that question. He had a Jesus tattoo across his finger, and he'd mentioned his faith a couple times.

"I do. I prefer a smaller congregation. But Chloe likes bigger churches where she can have lots of friends. At the church we've been attending, there's only one other little girl her age."

"That would be difficult. You want kids to have good influences, right?"

"I do. But Mike and Sandy are very popular in this area." He glanced up at the sign and frowned.

The edge to his voice made me wonder.

I didn't really have time to ask him about it, though. We pulled up to the Oleander Resort.

My heart pounded against my ribcage as I stared at the well-landscaped grounds. Not just because of what happened yesterday, but because this was the place my father had worked when he died. Now, it seemed even more menacing.

It seemed like a hideout for trouble and danger.

What would our visit hold for us today?

AS I STEPPED out of the minivan, I paused. A shiver went up my spine as I surveyed the area.

Was that person watching me again? The one who always seemed to be a few steps behind, monitoring my every move?

I didn't have that feeling now. But the fact that I never knew when this feeling might pop up left me on edge. How long could I live like this?

"Are you okay?" Michael had somehow appeared right beside me, asking his familiar question.

"It's just weird to be here." I crossed my arms over my chest, trying to ward away the chill that started at my core. "Yesterday, I was distracted by the whole lip-synching competition, so I didn't dwell so much on my father. But today, all I can think about is my dad and what happened to him here."

Michael offered a compassionate frown. "You said he worked here?"

I nodded, staring at the building ahead of us. "He did. He went from a suit-wearing government job . . . to working buildings and grounds maintenance at this resort and waiting on rich people."

"I'm sure that would be quite the life change."

"He never complained about it, though. He said he would do whatever he could to help our family. And that's what he did. He went to work every day. He did his job, and he got his paycheck."

"Sometimes I think they don't make people like that anymore, you know?"

I nodded.

Michael studied my face. "You said he died of a heart attack?"

A tinge of guilt nagged at me for not telling the whole truth. But as far as everybody knew, that *was* how my father died. It said so on his death certificate.

So it wasn't a lie. Not exactly. It just wasn't the whole story … maybe.

"His boss called me one day. He wasn't able to get in contact with my mom, and I was the backup number. He told me that my father had a heart attack and was on his way to the hospital. I could tell by his voice that it wasn't good. By the time we got to the hospital, he was already gone."

Michael squeezed my shoulder, and his voice softened as he said, "I'm sorry. I know that had to be really difficult."

I held back the tears that sprung into my eyes. "I find a lot of comfort in knowing he's in a better place right now. I just wish that this wasn't the way it ended, you know? I wish that he'd been able to get back on his feet. To see my sister get her lung transplant. To know that his family was okay."

"I can imagine how hard that must be on you."

I cleared my throat, realizing I'd gotten a lot more personal than I'd intended. I needed to focus on right now instead of dwelling on the past. I dropped my arms to my sides and drew in a deep breath.

"Listen, how about if we go inside and see if we can find out anything? I'm taking a trip down the River of Sad, and there's a waterfall at the end."

"What?"

"It's a Yerbian expression."

"Got it."

I was so thankful I had Michael by my side as we started toward the front door.

I still might go over that waterfall, and Michael might be the lifeguard I needed.

<h1 style="text-align:center">CHAPTER SEVEN</h1>

FIFTEEN MINUTES LATER, Michael and I were seated with the head of security, a man named Bruno Davis. I was pretty sure the only reason anyone at the resort was talking to us was because we worked for Oscar. I could be thankful for that because these people didn't have to talk to us at all.

Despite the tough name, Bruno was on the scrawnier side, with a completely bald head and a voice that was more high pitched than I'd expected. The man also wore two small hearing aids.

He'd explained when we met him that he'd been in the military and a bomb had exploded nearby while he served overseas. He'd lost 50 percent of his hearing and 100 percent of his career.

Bruno's office was a dark room with a wall filled with TV screens that monitored every area of the building. From a little board at his fingertips, he could zoom in and out from every angle.

"The police have already been here, and they've already been through this footage," Bruno explained, moving an old coffee mug out of the way.

Michael and I sat in two foldout chairs behind him.

"I understand," Michael said. "But Elliot has a personal connection to our victim, and we're hoping to find some answers for her."

"I was back here monitoring things when the video feed went down," Bruno said. "I've been telling management for a while that we need to upgrade our security."

"Would someone be able to control the cameras remotely?" Michael said.

"It's the only thing that makes sense," Bruno said. "We need more firewalls in place. Hackers keep getting smarter faster than we can keep things updated."

"That is a problem," I muttered.

"Here's the problem." Bruno pulled up his computer and tilted the screen until we could see it better. "This is about ten minutes before this man died. As you can see, he stepped into the building through an exit door that someone propped open."

"Who propped it open?" I asked, my eyes glued to the video.

The footage was fairly high quality, but it had been

recorded at an odd angle. I mostly saw a sea of bobbing heads. There appeared to be too many people for the space.

"One of the participants opened it," Bruno said. "Said he got hot. If he thinks this is hot, he should try Iraq."

"Thanks for your service to our country." Michael offered a nod before getting back to business and pointing to the time stamp at the bottom of the screen. "That would be right about the time we were waiting backstage to go on."

I nodded. The timeline matched.

"What next?" Michael asked.

Bruno pointed at the screen. "Our victim stepped inside and stood against the wall watching everybody. Nobody said anything to him or even looked at him, for that matter. It was like the man was a ghost or invisible or something."

"And then?" I could hardly wait to know what happened next.

I assumed that if the police had seen the killer, that Hunter would have said something . . . which left me wondering exactly what *did* happen next.

Bruno frowned and leaned back in his chair. "That's when our camera footage went down. We've searched any and everything. The footage from the time of the murder isn't there. Someone stopped it from being recorded."

I shook my head in disbelief. "Do you have any idea who?"

"I have no idea." Bruno sighed. "We're looking into it. The

problem is *all* of our cameras went down at some point during the time of the murder, not just that one."

"How convenient." Michael shook his head and leaned back, his jaw flexing while he thought.

"Exactly." Bruno looked equally as disgusted.

I leaned forward, my mind still racing. "How many people at this resort know where those cameras are and how they're operated?"

"We have about ten employees who work security. But, if we count everybody, about thirty people have worked for our security department over the past three years. A lot of times, we get college kids who come for the summer. It makes it seem like we have a lot more turnover than we actually do."

"I'm assuming the police got the names of all those people?" Michael asked.

"They did." Bruno nodded. "But any of our former employees could share camera information with any of their friends. I think the pool of people who have this information is a lot bigger than those thirty people. All of our employees know about the importance of keeping confidential information confidential. If I find out somebody on my staff has been sharing things that they shouldn't, they're out of here."

The man's voice left no doubt that he spoke the truth.

"Do you mind if I take a cell phone video of the man coming in through that door?" I asked. "I'd like to review it."

Bruno glanced at the door to his office, which was barely cracked open. "What I don't see, I can't say anything about."

He rewound the footage. As he did, I pulled out my phone and recorded it.

I knew Hunter probably wouldn't give us the actual footage. And, if he did, we'd have to jump through hoops to do so. This seemed like a good alternative.

When I was done recording, Michael and I stood, ready to leave. But Bruno called my name before I left his office.

"Your dad worked here, didn't he?"

My breath caught. I hadn't said my last name. As far as I knew, Bruno had no idea about my relationship with my dad. So how had he found out that information?

After a moment of thought, I nodded. "He did. How do you know that?"

"You look like him," Bruno said. "I can hear the subtle accent in your voice."

"So you knew my dad?" That realization threw me off. Papa hadn't been in the country long enough to make that many friends. Honestly, I knew so little about his time here. I'd been too consumed with my own problems.

"I didn't know him well. But he seemed like a good man. In fact, we were having some problems with one of our employees here breaking into the office to steal petty cash, and your dad helped us to figure out who was behind it. He seemed to have a knack for those kinds of things."

A burst of pride went through me. I could totally see my dad doing that. I was glad he had made a good impression in the short time he was here.

"I was really sorry about his heart attack," Bruno continued, his weathered face lined with compassionate grief. "It was a big loss for us here, but I can only imagine it was a bigger loss for you and your family."

My throat tightened. "Thank you. It was. We miss him very much."

As Michael and I headed toward the door, Michael murmured in my ear, "Your dad sounds like quite the man."

"You two would have probably gotten along well."

We stepped from the room, and I opened my mouth to discuss what we'd learned. Before I could, Palmer, the resort manager, found us.

Had he been waiting outside the room for us? Had he heard any part of our conversation?

"I was hoping to catch you and see how things went," Palmer started. "Did I hear that you're Eduardo's daughter?"

"I am."

"I'm sorry for your loss also. I've got to say that nobody from the family ever came to get the things that he left in his locker."

"What?" The question escaped before I could stop it. "What locker?"

"Nobody told you?" Palmer's eyes narrowed with confusion. "We all have lockers here. Your father's was never emptied. I pulled his things out, waiting for someone to come retrieve them. My secretary was supposed to leave a message for you."

Everything else around me seemed to disappear. "Where are they now?"

"I left them in the resort safe." He paused. "I almost put them in my office, but I guess it's a good thing I didn't. A few days after he passed, we had a break-in here at the resort. All my things were riffled through. I'm not sure if his things would have stayed together or been strewn and counted as collateral damage."

Was that a coincidence? Or had someone been looking for something in connection to my father?

"Who has access to the safe?" I asked.

"Just me and my assistant manager."

"Is there any way I could get those things now?" My throat burned as I said the words.

"Let's see if we can make it happen."

I wasn't sure if I was more excited or more nervous as I anticipated what I might find in my dad's possessions.

MICHAEL REMAINED beside me as I stood at a desk with a bag full of my dad's things. This room was normally used by business-minded guests. There were several offices that could be reserved for those who needed them.

I was thankful for the privacy.

I couldn't believe it was the first time I'd heard about my

father's locker and that nobody at the resort had bothered to let my family know.

I had no idea what might be inside the grocery-sized paper bag. It could be nothing . . . or it could be everything.

"Are you sure you want to do this here?" Michael placed his hand over mine, stopping me before I opened the bag.

The warmth in his touch caused a shiver to run down my spine. Or maybe it was just the emotions of this situation. I couldn't be sure.

"I'm sure." I couldn't wait a moment longer.

What I wasn't sure about is whether or not Michael should be here with me.

I had no idea what I was about to discover.

Despite that, I tugged at the sides of the bag until the staples holding it shut pulled open. Gingerly, I opened the paper folds.

Then I looked inside.

Tears welled in my eyes as I pulled out my dad's favorite shirt. I held it to my face and took in a deep breath.

It smelled like chicory, dried leaves, and grass clippings—all the things that reminded me of my dad.

It took every ounce of my energy to hold myself together as I reached down and pulled out the next item.

Michael's hand went to my shoulder as if he could sense the emotions raging inside me. I appreciated his thoughtfulness.

I drew in a deep breath before lifting up my dad's hat.

He'd loved wearing the floppy, khaki-colored accessory. He'd always talked about how practical it was.

There were also some pictures of the family that Papa must have hung up inside his locker. Some sunscreen. Some Chapstick.

And that was it.

Why did I feel so unsettled knowing that? I supposed part of me had wanted more. I'd been hoping that maybe my dad left me some type of clue.

That wasn't the case.

"Are you sure you're okay?" Michael leaned toward me, his hands pressed against the desktop.

I nodded and ran my fingers across my dad's shirt again. "I guess so. I just didn't expect . . ."

"I know." Michael's voice sounded sincere and compassionate. "I know."

I began putting everything back in the bag, realizing I shouldn't draw this out any longer. "I guess we can go now."

As I lifted his hat, something fell to the floor.

My heart quickened as I bent down to find what fell. My fingers closed over a small metal stick.

I raised it into the air.

It was a jump drive.

What in the world would Papa be doing with this?

CHAPTER EIGHT

"WHAT SHOULD I DO WITH THIS?" I stared at the jump drive, my heart thumping with anticipation.

"You should see what's on it," Michael said. "You think it's . . . something bad?"

I reminded myself that Michael thought my dad died of a heart attack.

"I just . . . don't have any idea what this could be," I finally said, pulling my gaze up to meet his. "Family photos? Or maybe it's just work stuff."

"Was it like your dad to carry around a jump drive?"

I shook my head, not even having to think about my answer. "No, it wasn't. I'm not even sure where it came from."

"It could have fallen out of his shirt or something."

"I suppose." But I had a sneaking suspicion that the device had been hidden somewhere within his garments. I could hardly breathe as I anticipated what I might learn if I accessed this.

Michael pulled the backpack from his shoulders and set it on the desk. "No pressure, but I have my laptop with me."

My heart continued to beat, beat, beat in my ears. "Do you?"

If Michael helped me access this, he could learn stuff I didn't intend for him to know. I had to make a quick choice: let him get involved or put this off until later.

However, I knew that Michael had a better chance of figuring this jump drive out than I did. Technology wasn't my thing.

My throat burned as I looked at him and nodded. "Okay…"

"You sure?" He tilted his head.

I nodded again. "Positive."

He pulled out his laptop and placed in on the desk. Then he extended his hand, waiting for the jump drive. After a moment of hesitation, I placed the device in his palm.

Please don't make me regret this and make my heart feel amiss. There's so much at stake. I'm tired of being fake. How much more of this can I take?

Michael slipped the jump drive into the computer and waited.

I held my breath as the seconds ticked past.

Michael tapped his hand against the desk as the computer tried to open the device.

Why was this taking so long? Or was I especially impatient today? I wasn't normally an impatient person. But anticipation zinged through my blood.

Michael let out a grunt and leaned closer to the screen.

"What is it?" I asked, barely able to breathe.

"It's encrypted. We need a four-digit code to access it."

"What?" My father had known how to do stuff like that? Since he *was* a spy, I shouldn't be surprised.

Michael glanced at me, his expression calm. "Any guesses? You probably have three chances before you get locked out."

Pressure continued to mount inside me. What would my father have used?

His anniversary! It made the most sense.

"Try zero six one two," I said.

Michael typed in the digits.

The computer dinged, indicating we were wrong.

"Two more guesses," Michael said.

I stared at the wall. What would Papa have used? His birthday? My mom's? Mine? My sister's? There were too many options and not enough chances to try them all.

"I'm going to need to think about it," I finally said, running a hand through my hair.

"Probably a good idea." He pulled the jump drive out and handed it back to me before putting away his computer. "It was worth a shot, right?"

I nodded, still feeling like my head was spinning as I slipped the device into my pocket. "Yes, it was."

"I have a friend who's pretty good at cracking stuff like that. I could take it to him, if you want."

Did I want that? Part of me didn't want to let this jump drive out of my sight. It was practically burning a hole in my jeans right now.

"Let me think about it," I finally said.

"Of course." Michael stood and heaved his bag back onto his shoulder. "For now, I think we should get out of here."

"Sounds good."

As we stepped toward the door, questions swirled in my head. I needed some time alone to sort through this. It was an introvert thing.

I tugged on the door handle, but it didn't budge.

"What's wrong?" Michael asked.

"I can't open this."

He stepped beside me and tugged on it also. It didn't move for him either.

"This is weird," he muttered.

Just as he said the words, smoke begin creeping in from under the doorway.

The two of us exchanged a glance.

"What are we going to do?" I muttered.

"We need to get out of here." Michael glanced around. "Take your sweater off. Stuff it under the door."

I didn't ask any questions. I did what Michael said and shoved the sweater as far as I could into the crack.

As I did, Michael pounded on the door. "Help! We need help in here!"

I stood, alarm still coursing through me as the air thickened.

"Call the front desk," Michael barked. "See if they can send someone down here!"

My hands trembled as I grabbed my phone. I quickly dialed the number, praying someone would answer.

They didn't.

I glanced down. Some smoke still crept beneath the door.

What was going on? Was there a fire out there?

I touched the door. It wasn't hot.

So where was the smoke coming from?

Michael pounded at the door again. "Help! We need help in here!"

Still, no one came.

"Try your phone again," Michael said.

I dialed the front desk again.

Still no answer.

I coughed as the smoke irritated my lungs. Quickly, I pulled my shirt over my mouth, trying to protect my lungs for as long as I could.

I did a quick search and found an alternate number— direct to Palmer Birmingham. His secretary answered.

Yes!

"This is Elliot Ransom. I'm trapped in a spare office here at the Oleander. The door is jammed, and smoke is creeping inside. We need help. Now!"

"What?" the secretary asked.

I told her again, more slowly this time.

"We'll get someone right down there," she said. "Hang tight."

As more smoke filled the space, Michael took my arm and led me away from the door. He pushed on each of the windows, but nothing happened. They were all sealed, probably for safety purposes. Later, I'd consider how ironic that was.

For now, I needed to keep searching for a way out of this situation.

"There's got to be something else we can do," Michael muttered, still glancing around.

I hoped help got here soon because I could hardly breathe and more smoke filled the air.

CHAPTER NINE

JUST AS ANOTHER coughing fit seized me, I heard someone outside the door.

Was that some kind of spray? A fire extinguisher?

I couldn't be sure.

The smoke made the entire room hazy.

"It's going to be okay," Michael said, pulling his own shirt over his nose as he glanced around.

He was still looking for a way out. Just in case, I supposed.

How much longer could we make it in here with this smoke?

"We need to get down low," Michael said. "Smoke rises."

We dropped down to our knees.

He was right. My eyes didn't sting quite as much. But I wasn't sure how much longer I'd be able to say that.

What was going on outside our door? I'd thought for sure help was here.

I coughed again, wondering if this was what my sister always felt like with her lung condition.

Finally, the door flung open.

Palmer and Bruno rushed inside.

Bruno grabbed our arms and pulled us into the hallway before asking, "Are you okay?"

"I think so," Michael said, coughing again and waving a hand in front of his face as some smoke lingered.

As we stood there, I remembered the jump drive in my pocket.

All of this had happened when I found it. Was someone trying to scare me off? Trying to get their hands on it?

I had no idea.

But I knew things had just taken another turn for the worse.

"What happened?" Michael asked, glancing around for the source of our distress.

"It looked like someone lit a fire starter and shoved it under the door," Bruno said. "And someone jammed the lock somehow."

I glanced down and saw that a jacket had been thrown over something on the floor. Using my foot, I nudged the material. Sure enough, a little stick was there, smoke coming from its stem.

"I'm so sorry this happened while you were in our care

here." Palmer frowned as he studied us. "Are the two of you really okay?"

The man looked sincerely concerned as he waited for our response.

I nodded. "I think so."

But, as if to betray my words, another coughing fit hit me.

I looked up just in time to see another familiar figure in the background.

It was Headset Guy.

He stared at us in the distance before darting away.

Just seeing him right now made my blood go cold.

I TRIED to push down my anxiety as Michael and I walked toward the resort exit. Palmer had called and filed a report with the police. While he did that, Bruno had checked the security footage.

The whole security system had gone down again.

Unease churned in my stomach. Someone knew exactly what they were doing. They'd planned their moves carefully. Not only that, but this killer was on the ball enough that he was also opportunistic.

He couldn't have known Michael and I would be at the Oleander today. But he'd noticed, and he'd jumped at the chance to try to stop us.

What was I going to do now?

I had to make some choices, but I didn't want to rush them. Still, the unknown made me feel like I was being ripped apart inside.

"You sure you're okay?" Michael asked.

"Yeah, but that was crazy," I said, rubbing my neck. My throat still burned from the smoke. "Someone doesn't want us investigating, do they?"

"I'd say. They were willing to kill us to ensure that."

I glanced at him in surprise. "You really think that was the goal?"

"Considering the fact that our only exit was on fire? I'd say yes."

I shivered. This just kept getting worse and worse.

As we stepped outside the resort, I spotted a landscaper working in the flowerbeds near the entrance. He was probably in his sixties, with a shock of white hair, weathered skin, and a lean build. He wore coveralls and had his tools spread out around him—a small shovel, gardening shears, and a hand trowel.

He glanced over at Michael and me, doing a double take when his gaze fell on me.

Did he recognize me?

The man didn't look familiar to me at all.

But I couldn't leave here without finding out some answers. If this man recognized me, I wanted to know why.

I paced toward him as he rearranged some potted flowers he was about to plant. He seemed to sense my presence because, before I even said anything, he murmured, "I can't decide exactly how to lay them out."

"If you want them evenly spaced out, you need to move that one on the left over about two inches. And this one over here needs to come forward three inches, I'd say."

The man glanced at me. "You really have an eye for stuff like this, don't you?"

"I'm slightly obsessed with things being symmetrical."

"That's a true fact," Michael added.

"Don't I know you?" The man studied my face even more. "You looked familiar when you walked out, but I'm not sure why."

I briefly contemplated how much to say before announcing, "I don't think you know me, but maybe you knew my father. He used to work here."

Realization stretched across his gaze. "Eduardo?"

I nodded. "That's him."

A smile lit the man's face, and, the next instant, he pulled me into a hug. The scent of dirt, fertilizer, and pungent cologne filled my senses.

"Of course. You're his daughter," the man muttered. "You're his spitting image."

The hug only lasted a moment before the man stepped back, his eyes still glimmering with grief and realization.

"I'm Dennis, by the way. Dennis Haskell."

"I'm Elliot. And this is my friend, Michael." I drew in a

breath, wondering exactly where this conversation would go. "So you and my father worked together?"

"We did. He was a hard worker. I never had to worry about him not doing what he said. I can't say that for a lot of people here."

"How long have you worked here, Dennis?" Michael asked. His voice sounded casual, but I knew he was prodding for information.

"About seven years."

"Did you, by chance, hear about the man who died yesterday at the lip-synch competition?" I asked.

Dennis brushed some dirt from his hands and crossed his arms over his chest as he turned to us, his work forgotten for a minute. "It's been all the talk here today. Nobody can believe it."

"There any rumors going around as to what might have happened?" Michael asked.

"Not really. It's all a big mystery."

"I understand," I said. "It was really nice to meet you."

Dennis gazed at me for a moment longer, almost as if he wanted to say something else.

I made no effort to move, just in case whatever was on his mind was relevant.

"I am sorry your dad was dealing with so much stress before he died. I only hope it didn't cause his heart attack."

My back went ramrod straight. What was this man talking about?

CHAPTER TEN

"WHAT DO YOU MEAN?" I asked as Dennis's words reverberated in my head.

I'm sorry your dad was dealing with so much stress before he died . . .

"The day before your father died, I saw some men confront him over there." Dennis nodded toward the golf course in the distance. "I don't know what they were talking about, but it was heated."

Michael squeezed closer. "How many men were there?"

"Three men."

"Had you ever seen them before?" My mind raced along with my pulse.

"I hadn't. They were far away, so I couldn't see very well."

"Could you describe them?" Maybe *this* was the information I'd been searching for.

"I don't know. They looked Hispanic, if I had to guess. They were dressed nice, more like businesspeople than people who were out golfing."

Hispanic? Had they been from Yerba? "You didn't hear anything they said?"

Dennis frowned. "No, I'm sorry. I wish I had. It sounds like you didn't know about any of this."

There was a lot I didn't appear to know about. My dad's locker. The jump drive. This argument with three mystery men.

Exactly what was going on in my dad's life before he died?

It seemed a shame that I'd been in the dark about so much. How would I ever find answers?

"Thank you so much for your help, Dennis," I said. "I really appreciate it."

"No problem."

Michael didn't say anything until we got into the van and locked the doors. Then he turned to me, his eyes probing mine. "You look like you've seen a ghost."

I needed to pull myself together before I gave away more information than I should. "It's just hard talking about my father still."

"Is that all?" Michael studied me, probably looking for any signs of deceit.

I was sure I was showing plenty. My body fidgeting. My eyes shifting. My skin sweating.

Michael was using his investigative skills on me, wasn't he?

I had to keep my cool before I gave away more than I intended. "Yeah. What else could it be?"

He stared at me another moment before shrugging. "You seem concerned about these men your father was arguing with."

"Wouldn't you be? I definitely don't like the idea of anyone harassing my father while he was on the job."

Michael leaned back, in no hurry to leave. "Was that like your dad? Did he like to argue with people?"

"When he needed to argue, he would. But he was also smart. He knew how to handle situations. I watched my dad turn heated arguments into a moment of camaraderie in the blink of an eye. He had that gift, a way of phrasing things in such a way that it would spin the conversation into an entirely different direction."

"He sounds like quite a guy."

I felt the sad smile tugging at my lips. "He was. He definitely was."

Michael shifted, that compassionate expression present in his gaze.

"So what now?" I asked Michael, trying to keep my mind off my father. "Any other ideas on how to figure out what happened to this mystery man who died yesterday?"

"There's one other person that I'd like to talk to."

I jerked my head toward Michael, surprised by his

response. I'd halfway expected him to feel as clueless and lost as I did. "Who's that?"

"One of our competitors who was backstage when the victim walked in through that exit door."

"There were a lot of people back there," I said.

"I know, but this man, in particular, glanced at the victim when he walked in. Maybe he saw something."

"And you know who this man is and where to find him?"

"He works at The Burger Joint," Michael said. "I think we should pay him a visit."

"I'm up for anything. We still haven't heard from Oscar about working Marla's case, right?"

"No, but I texted Velma. Oscar and Marla have gone to have lunch together, so we still have time."

"All right then. Let's talk to this guy at The Burger Joint."

AS SOON AS we walked into The Burger Joint, I recognized the man Michael wanted to speak with.

The college-aged boy was a regular showtunes kind of guy from what I remembered about him backstage. In fact, the short, thin man seemed like the type who could hop up on the table at any minute to put on a song and dance.

As soon as he saw us, he came over with two menus in hand. Happy strands of "Great Balls of Fire" rang through the system, and the scent of burgers and fries filled the air.

"Table for two?" Even the server's voice had a singsong quality about it.

"We were actually hoping that we could ask you a few questions about what happened at the lip-synching competition," Michael said.

The man's smile faltered but only for a minute. "Of course. You two were there also, weren't you? You look familiar."

"We're with Driscoll and Associates," Michael said.

His eyes widened. "The PI firm? Whatever I can do to help the situation. How about if I get you some drinks?"

A few minutes later, Michael and I were seated in a booth. I had gotten a limeade, while Michael got a Coke, and the showtunes employee sipped on a milkshake while on a quick break.

"So what can I help you with? My name is Pinky, by the way."

"Pinky?" There was no hiding the surprise in Michael's eyes.

"I know." He shrugged, no sign of embarrassment. "It's a nickname. What can I say?"

Michael shifted in his seat. "Tell me, did you see the man who died when he first slipped backstage?"

"No, I'm sorry to say I didn't. But you know how crowded it was backstage. It was hard to see anything." He took a sip of his drink, his over-the-top expression almost comical.

"I'm sure the police have already talked to you," I said.

"Did you see anything strange when you were back there? Anything at all?"

Pinky rested his elbows on the table. "No, I wish I did. I thought about it all night last night, trying to think if there was something I missed. But I came up as empty as those chairs at the empty tables in *Les Mis*."

What? I didn't ask.

"It's funny because, in the video, it's like you're looking right at the man when he slipped inside the exit door," I said. "In fact, I am pretty sure you were the one who propped it open when you got back there, weren't you?"

Pinky's face lost a little bit of its color. "I did prop the door open. But obviously, I had no idea that someone was going to sneak inside and then die."

"So did you or didn't you see that man before he was stabbed to death?" I needed to get to the truth of the matter and couldn't afford to mince any words.

Pinky's face twisted in confusion. "I thought I *might* have seen him. In fact, I wondered if I should shut the door, for safety reasons and all. When I glanced back over, I thought I saw someone standing by the door. I didn't recognize the man, nor did he seem to be socializing with anybody nor like the lip-synching type. I figured he was with the resort."

"And then?" Michael rested his muscular arms on the table as he waited for a response.

Or was he subtly threatening the man by showing his strength? I wasn't sure.

Pinky shrugged before taking another sip of his shake. "And then nothing. The leader of our Burger Combo—that's what we called ourselves—called us so we did some warm-up vocal exercises. I didn't think anything else about the guy until I heard somebody scream."

"You're sure you don't know anything else?" Michael leaned closer, his gaze narrowed.

"I'm sure. I'm sorry. I wish I could tell you more, but I can't." Pinky glanced at his watch. "Now, it looks like my break is up. Sorry I couldn't be more help. But I am hoping the lip-synching competition is going to be rescheduled. We've gotten number one for the past two years, and I'm hoping to be number one again."

Without saying anything else, Pinky popped up from the booth and went back to work.

Michael and I looked at each other. Neither of us had to say anything to know what the other was thinking.

This lead had been a waste of time.

But at least I'd gotten a limeade out of it.

CHAPTER ELEVEN

MICHAEL and I stepped out of The Burger Joint, our clothes covered in a fresh coat of grease and our ears ringing from the loud music.

We paused in front of the place and turned to each other, taking a moment to speak without any listening ears.

"So, what do you think?" As I asked the question, the wind kicked up and strands of hair slapped my face. Rain was in the forecast for this evening.

"I don't know." Michael crossed his arms and stared down the street in thought. "Somebody backstage had to have seen something."

"I agree. Someone just doesn't get killed in a roomful of people with no one around to see anything. Although . . . I have to say everybody backstage *was* pretty distracted with their upcoming performances."

"True fact."

"Maybe we're talking to the wrong people," I suggested. "We're talking to a guy who seems to have ADHD. Maybe we need to talk to somebody who has a job that requires more attention to detail."

"Maybe someone at the boutique?"

I nodded. "They might be a better choice. I know the police have probably already spoken with them, but it can't hurt to prod a bit more, right?"

"Now you're starting to think like an investigator. Good job."

I felt myself beaming.

Michael stared at my face for a minute. "I have to admit that what bugs me the most about this is the fact that the victim had your name and your photo on him, Elliot. That's what I can't make sense of. You've only worked a few cases for Oscar, not enough to make that many enemies. The few you have made are awaiting trial. So who could this be?"

I tried to carefully consider my answer. Part of me wanted to spill everything as we stood there. I had to use some restraint here. "That's a great question. I am not really sure."

"There's nothing else you want to tell me?" His scrutiny grew deeper, like he was just begging me to open up.

There was so much I wanted to tell him. That jump drive felt like a thorn pressing into my skin, constantly nagging me with its presence.

My throat burned as I said, "Not really."

I would be wise to keep the information about my father close. The more people who knew, the more people who might use that against me.

It didn't stop the guilt from flooding me. How could I even say I considered Michael a friend when I was keeping this from him? On the other hand, keeping it from him might keep him safe.

Was I just using that as an excuse? Nothing seemed black-and-white anymore. I wished it did.

As I glanced over Michael's shoulder, I saw a man on the corner. He leaned against the building, looking at his cell phone. Every once in a while, he glanced up at Michael and me.

The realization caused my back muscles to stiffen.

"What's wrong?" Michael asked.

"Don't make any sudden moves, but I think that man back there is watching us."

Michael pulled out his phone. He unlocked it and put his camera on selfie mode so he could see over his shoulder.

I made a mental note of that tip. I could use all the tips I could get when it came to these things.

But as soon as Michael moved, the man spooked and darted in the opposite direction.

MICHAEL and I took off after the man.

But our watcher had too much of a head start.

"Hey!" Michael yelled.

Did that ever actually work? Definitely not this time.

The man sprinted around the corner and out of sight.

As we turned onto the street, I stopped.

The man was . . . gone.

He couldn't have given us the slip that easily.

Michael kept running, obviously more well-versed in these types of things than I was. Stopping wouldn't help us find this guy.

Michael reached an alley and paused. I caught up, but Michael raised a hand, halting me before I could run into the area.

"We need to be careful," he muttered. "We don't know where this guy is. We don't want him to take us by surprise."

I sucked in a deep breath, my lungs crying out for air. It was times like this that I wished I wasn't such a spelling bee-loving, symmetry-obsessed bookworm and was more of a hardcore, sweat-producing, pain-devoted athlete instead.

I stayed behind Michael as he crept forward, surveying the area around us.

There were probably nine different cars back here. But no one was in sight.

The small lot was surrounded by three- and four-story buildings. A couple of dumpsters and various boxes sat by the back entrance to one restaurant.

If I were this man, where would I be hiding right now?

There were almost too many options for my comfort. Too many places to hide. To plan for a surprise attack.

Michael motioned for me to remain against the wall of one of the businesses. As we crept alongside it, I listened.

I hoped to hear some type of telltale sign about where the man was.

In an instant, an image of the dead man from yesterday filled me. I remembered the wound to his abdomen. I remembered the sickly, pale expression on his dead face.

If Michael and I weren't careful, that could be us.

Michael pushed his hand back, making sure I remained behind him and that he was in front, ready to take the brunt of anything that was about to happen.

It was the last thing I wanted. If Michael got hurt because of me . . . I would never forgive myself.

I glanced around again.

That man had to be back here. It was the only place that made sense. The only other area he could have gone was straight ahead. In that case, we would have seen him.

Carefully, we crept forward.

We'd almost reached the end of the first building.

I scanned the area in between each of the cars. By the dumpster. Near those boxes.

I saw no one.

As the seconds ticked past, a rhyme formed in my mind.

I don't want to be a drama queen. But I feel like I'm going to get creamed. Just where did this guy go? And why was he our foe?

Would we survive this? I didn't know, but I hoped the answer wasn't . . . no.

Was that a double negative?

It didn't matter right now.

Just then, an engine roared to life.

My eyes widened when I saw a black sedan start forward.

The vehicle charged right for us.

And there was nowhere for us to go.

Just a building behind us, trapping us.

That car was going to hit us, I realized.

What were we going to do?

CHAPTER TWELVE

"ELLIOT!" Michael yelled.

Before I realized what was happening, he threw himself over me. We both flew through the air before landing on the sidewalk.

Somehow, Michael managed to turn in midair, allowing his body to take the brunt of the fall. I landed on top of him, and his arms went around me. He turned me until I was against the wall, and his body blocked me from the car.

When the car was only a foot away, the driver swerved to the left. The tires squealed as the car sped away.

My heart pounded out of control.

That man had tried to kill us. Had almost succeeded. Thank goodness for Michael's quick thinking.

Michael let out a groan and turned to me, his eyes orbs of

concern as he studied me for any sign of injury. "Elliot . . . are you okay?"

As I pushed myself up on the rough asphalt, an ache pulsed in my shoulder.

It was nothing I wouldn't get over.

"I'm fine." I rubbed my shoulder. "How about you?"

I quickly scanned Michael, looking for any signs of injury. He sat up and rolled his shoulders back, his face twisting in a moment of discomfort.

"I've been through worse," he said. "That was close."

"Tell me about it." I stared at Michael for another moment, making sure he truly was okay. I had a strange urge to reach forward and touch the side of his face to let him know how much I appreciated him saving my life.

But that would be weird. People didn't touch their coworkers' faces. I supposed that people didn't even do that with their friends.

With that insight, I forced my hands to remain at my side.

Michael pushed himself to his feet, still trying to work out the stiffness from the fall. He reached down for my hand and pulled me to my feet also.

"Did you notice anything in particular about the car?" he asked, back to being all business.

"It was a black Audi. Tinted windows. It almost looked like there was some kind of screen over the license plate, so I couldn't get a good read on it."

"That's what I thought too." He frowned. "I don't know

who that person was, but he seems to know what he's doing. I don't think he was your run-of-the-mill criminal."

"If he was able to kill that man at the lip-synching competition without anybody seeing him, then I'm inclined to agree." I sighed and glanced around one more time. "What now?"

Michael looked at his phone. "Now, Oscar wants to see us back in the office. I guess it's time to start working on the Marla Burns case."

That just seemed like such a letdown after everything that happened today. "Should we call the police first? File a report?"

Michael frowned. "I guess we should."

But I could read the subtext of what he was telling me. We still had work to do outside of this.

But I couldn't deny that a part of me felt disappointed that we wouldn't be able to look into this more. Not right now, at least.

But I realized more than ever, somebody was definitely watching me. I didn't know why, but I did know they were ready to kill me at the first opportunity.

BACK IN THE OFFICE, Oscar reviewed with us all of the details of the Marla Burns case. Then Michael and I split up and looked into the backgrounds of various people Marla had put on her suspect list. Mostly, we were trying to confirm locations of each of the men for the time of the deliveries.

In some cases, that was easy. The suspects lived out of the state or they were at jobs or had standing appointments.

We should be able to eliminate probably about half of Marla's list just by doing the research first.

My mind was only halfway focused, though. I couldn't stop thinking about the jump drive. What was on it? Should I trust Michael's friend to possibly unlock it?

I also couldn't stop thinking about the dead man. About who he was. About who could have killed him.

Whoever it was, the man who'd killed him wasn't giving up. Today's events had made that clear.

That thought didn't make me feel any better.

Another question also lingered. Which man was the bad guy? The man who'd died or the man who'd killed him.

At five o'clock, it was time to go home. Michael and I would pick this up tomorrow with another stakeout.

Yay, she said with fake enthusiasm.

Michael walked me to my car, his steps slower than usual. "After everything that's happened, I feel like I should drive you home."

"I'll be fine."

He gave me that half-tilted head look. "I wouldn't be so sure of that. Do you not remember everything that's happened?"

He had me on that point. "I know. But I'll be careful."

He stared at me another moment, almost as if he was hesitant to believe me. Or maybe it was because he wanted to leave me.

A rhyme?

Maybe I was more nervous than I thought.

Finally he nodded. "Well, do me a favor and call me when you get home at least?"

"Absolutely."

"It's a deal. Oh, and don't forget about Chloe's thing at school tomorrow. Are you still good to go?"

"I can't wait." I'd promised I'd fill in during a Muffins with Mom event at his daughter's elementary school. Chloe's grandma was out of town and couldn't attend.

"Great." Michael flashed a smile. "I'll see you in the morning, Elliot."

"Thanks, Michael. For everything."

I meant the words. He'd been a real lifesaver on more than one occasion.

I climbed into my car and cranked the engine. Fifteen minutes later, I pulled up to the little bungalow I called home. As soon as I did, I noticed the strange vehicle parked out front.

It wasn't a black Audi. No, it was a charcoal-gray truck with some ladders in the back.

Anything unusual had me on guard right now.

Maybe I would wait on texting Michael until I figured out who was here.

As I walked to the front door, I slid one key between each of my fingers, knowing I could use them as a weapon if I needed to. It was another trick my dad taught me.

Who was our visitor? What was on the other side of the door? I wished I wasn't on edge. But I felt like I was walking a ledge. Toughening up . . . that was my pledge.

Before I even stepped onto my front porch, the door opened.

I gripped my keys tighter and braced myself.

As a man stepped out of my house, I raised my hand, prepared to fight if it came down to it.

CHAPTER THIRTEEN

"ELLIOT." My mom stepped out behind the man. "You do remember Mr. Miller, don't you?"

Now that I had a better look at the man, he did look vaguely familiar.

I lowered my key-laden hand.

"Our landlord." My mom stared at me, sending a silent message to make a good impression.

"Of course," I muttered, letting out a self-conscious chuckle. Everything had me on edge lately, to the point where everyone was suspect in my mind.

"How are you, Elliot?" Mr. Miller walked down the steps and stood in front of me.

The man always seemed nice, like the happy type who never let things get to him. He was in his sixties with salt-

and-pepper hair and a big smile. That was the extent of what I knew about him.

"I'm doing fine, Mr. Miller. Long time no see."

He nodded at my mom. "Needed to come by to do an AC check. Soon it's going to be time to turn it on, and I needed to make sure it was working for you guys."

"We appreciate that." The rental house might not be much to look at, but it was efficient. I'd give him that.

"How are you lately, Elliot?" Mr. Miller stared at me a minute, concern in his voice.

"I can't complain," I said, although it was a lie. I had *so much* to complain about lately. I tried to stay positive, but today alone I *had* almost died—twice. Couldn't I give myself permission to whine, just a little?

"You're looking good." His face turned even more sober. "It's good to see that you guys are all hanging in after everything that happened."

Mr. Miller had known my dad. I wasn't really sure how the two of them were connected. I hadn't thought to ask back when my dad had been alive. But now I wondered if there was more to the story.

Of course, I couldn't ask those questions in front of my mom. Not without her becoming suspicious.

But what if Mr. Miller was the connection to my father I'd been looking for?

"If there's anything else you guys need, you let me know," he said. "Have a good evening."

With that, he walked out to his truck and pulled away.

I glanced at my mom, trying not to show anything in my gaze. But she had that intuition that always seemed to pick up on any discrepancies in my life. Changes in my lip gloss. Not taking my vitamins. Being secretly engaged.

Could she somehow sense that I had almost been killed again today?

I didn't know. Nor did I know if I should tell her that I'd been given some of my father's things today. I'd left the items —except for the jump drive—in the trunk of my car.

But I braced myself for whatever she was about to say.

"You look bedraggled."

I touched my hair then my face and shirt, trying to comprehend her words. "What do you mean *bedraggled*?"

I didn't think I'd ever heard my mom use that phrase before.

She had grown up here in the States, down in Georgia. But she'd left right after college to be a missionary in Yerba. That's where she had met my father. Every once in a while, certain Southern phrases escaped from her, things I'd never heard before.

"You look . . . you know . . . plumb tuckered."

I squinted. "You know I like plums, but . . ."

She shook her head. "I suppose I'm just saying that you look frazzled."

That made more sense. "Just another day on the job."

She scrutinized my face. "What exactly are they making

you do there at that law firm? And why do you smell like smoke?"

More guilt rose in me. The emotion was becoming a common companion to me lately. "Like I said, I'm kind of a peon there. So I'm the one who ends up doing errands and the things that nobody else wants to do. And the smoke? Someone must be burning leaves down the street."

"I see." She narrowed her eyes like she wanted to say more. But before she could, a car pulled up and my sister hopped out just in time for the car to pull away again.

My mom and I both stared at Ruth, our attention directed to her now.

I hadn't gotten a good glimpse of who the driver was, but he had pulled away entirely too fast for my comfort.

Before I could ask, my mom beat me to it.

"Who was that?" Mom asked, her eyes narrowed.

My sister shrugged and pulled her book bag up higher on her shoulder. "No one. Just a friend from school."

"A he or a she?" my mom continued.

My sister rolled her eyes. "He, if you must know."

"I don't like how he pulled away so quickly," my mom continued. "He could've at least walked you to the door."

"That's so old-fashioned."

I could tell my sister wanted to roll her eyes again, but she didn't. She knew what was best for her, obviously.

"You were out late studying, weren't you?" my mom continued.

"I had a lot of studying to do. What can I say?"

"Ruth Ransom, I don't like secrets."

At my mom's words, I felt my own cheeks flush. No, my mom didn't like lies. She wasn't going to be very happy with me when she found out I was keeping them also.

"Mom . . . there are no secrets," Ruth said, a little whine to her voice. "I went to school, and I had a study group, and now I'm home."

"I want you to start telling me where you are after school. I want names and numbers, in case I need to get in touch with you."

"Mama . . ." My sister's face pulled downward in a dramatic frown that was the crown of teenage angst.

"Don't *mama* me. I have enough on my mind without worrying more about you than I have to."

As the words left my mom's lips, my sister had another coughing fit. Worry pounded inside me.

"Can I just go inside and do my homework now?" Ruth stared at my mom. "Please? I'm tired, and I have a big test tomorrow."

"Sure, go inside. But I haven't forgotten about this conversation."

My sister gave me a look as she stomped past, almost as if she was either begging for my help or bitter that I'd been there to witness this.

But I had to agree with my mom on this one.

Sometimes I thought that my father's death was the

hardest on Ruth. She was still in high school, and she needed her dad right now more than anything. There was so much she was trying to navigate without him. Having a life-threatening illness was hard to swallow, even if you had grown up with that fact.

As my sister slipped inside, my mom turned to me. "I don't know what to do with that girl."

"Just be patient with her. We're all still trying to figure things out."

"I know." My mom frowned and ran her hand across her cheek.

I could tell she was trying not to cry in front of me. My heart broke at the thought of it. She shouldn't have to cry alone. But I knew that she wanted to be strong for my sister and me.

"I love you, Mama." I pulled her into a long hug.

When we pulled away, she quickly muttered, "I'm going to go hop in the shower."

I knew exactly what she was doing. Escaping so she could cry in private.

Before I could say anything to her, my phone rang. I glanced at the screen and realized it was Michael.

I was going to be in trouble. I hadn't called him yet, and he was obviously worried.

And it looked like I would have to wait on asking her about the items in my dad's locker.

As my mom disappeared inside, I put the phone to my ear. "Hey, Michael..."

CHAPTER FOURTEEN

THE NEXT MORNING, a rush of nerves swept through me as I stood outside the Storm River Elementary School.

I still wasn't exactly sure how I had ended up at Muffins with Mom. But I'd figured being here for Chloe was the least I could do. Chloe and I had gotten to know each other better this week when she'd come to lip-synching practices at the office in the evenings.

I wasn't sure why Oscar had waited so late to announce we'd be participating in the competition or to announce our song. But he had. We'd only rehearsed for four days before the competition.

The best part about those practices had been listening to Chloe's advice and observations on our routine. The girl was precocious and talkative and could handle conversations better than most adults.

I was meeting her at eight, and the event lasted an hour so I should be able to be at work by 9:30, at the latest.

I'd tried to dress respectably for the event, wearing my favorite jeans, a black shirt, and my Converse. It wasn't much, but I hoped it would work.

I saw Michael standing at the front door, and my steps slowed.

"What are you doing here?" I paused in front of him as parents hustled by with their kids.

His hands were shoved into the pockets of his jeans, and he had his usual casual look going on. Backward hat. Surfer-style loafers. A T-shirt with a redacted government memo on it.

"I thought I would wait around to say hello. I just dropped off Chloe a few minutes ago."

I had a feeling there was more to it than that. What wasn't he saying? "Were you afraid I wouldn't show?"

"You're Ms. Responsible. Of course, I thought you would show."

Then I realized what he was really doing here. Realization spread through me like wildfire in the Amazon. "You're afraid I brought trouble with me."

Michael said nothing, which was answer enough for me.

I had to admit there had been some strange things going on lately. I wasn't offended at the notion.

"If you don't want me to go inside, I totally understand." I tried to put myself in his shoes. If Chloe was my child, I would be cautious too—especially considering the fact that danger seemed to be following me.

"You're fine. Chloe is super excited to have you here. I just thought I would keep a lookout, you know." He tried to grin, but the action looked forced.

He was trying to play it off like it wasn't a big deal, but I could tell it was.

"Everyone needs someone to watch their back," I assured him, trying to put him at ease.

"So you're not weirded out?" He stared at me, waiting for my response.

"No, I'm not weirded out. I think it's sweet, actually."

He nodded, his shoulders softening some. "Thanks, Elliot. You're the best. Chloe's classroom is down the first hallway, the second door on the right."

"Got it."

He lowered his voice. "Thanks again for doing this. It's stuff like this that seems the hardest on Chloe. I usually think the two of us make a pretty good team together. But there are some occasions when I just can't be a mother and a father. She wants that female influence in her life."

Talking about stuff like this was the closest Michael came to opening up. I was honored that he trusted me enough to share that. "I'm happy to fill in. I just don't want to overstep."

"I appreciate that."

With a nod to each other, I stepped inside the school

building. I showed my ID, had my picture taken, and had to walk through a metal detector.

I almost felt like I was back in Yerba right as it was becoming a police state. But whatever it took to keep the kids safe, that was all that mattered.

As I headed to the office to sign in, I braced myself. I just needed to pretend like Chloe was Ruth, my little sister. I wasn't trying to be her mom. I was just trying to be a companion right now.

I hoped I didn't fail.

SO FAR, the Muffins with Mom was going smashingly well.

I really didn't have to talk very much. Instead, I just sat with Chloe, munched on a blueberry muffin, and sipped some orange juice served in a tiny Dixie cup. As I did, the teacher stood up front reading poems about moms and showing slideshows of the kids in class.

Chloe was practically glued to my side. The girl had a big smile and blonde hair— she looked nothing like Michael. I could only imagine what Chloe's mom must have looked like. No doubt, she was gorgeous. I saw Michael as the type who would go for that.

He had played professional baseball for a few years. Something had happened, and he'd given up that career.

Honestly, there was still so much I didn't know about the man.

As the teacher continued to talk, I glanced at the moms in the room. They made me realize I would never fit in a place like this. They all had designer clothes, shoes, and handbags.

Even if I had the money, I couldn't see myself spending that kind of cash on fashion.

Did that mean I would never find my place in Storm River?

After the teacher finished, we had approximately twenty more minutes to chat before class needed to start.

"I'm so glad you came today, Elliot," Chloe started. "Everybody else has their mom here, but I never do."

"I'm sorry." I squeezed her hand. "It's always hard to lose the people we love."

"I don't know if I love my mom or not. I don't even remember her at all. Do you think she loves me?" Chloe glanced at me, her eyes orbs of questions.

My heart pounded in my ears. I wasn't prepared for these kinds of conversations. I prayed for wisdom before answering.

"I'm sure she loves you, Chloe," I finally said. "Different people show their love in different ways, though. Sometimes we may not ever know exactly what they're thinking. We may not understand their actions. But I do know that a mother's love is strong."

She began to color a sheet in front of her as we talked. "Well, I have my dad. He's the best dad in the whole world."

I smiled at the affection in Chloe's voice. "He does seem like a pretty great dad."

"I think he gets lonely sometimes." Chloe frowned but kept filling in a flower outline on her sheet.

I held my breath. I wasn't sure if Michael would want her talking about this. Yet I didn't want to blow her off either.

"Is that right?" I finally said.

"I'm okay with him getting married. I want a baby brother one day."

"Not a baby sister?"

She shrugged. "I guess that would be okay. But I really want a baby brother."

Sadness pressed on me as I listened to her. Sometimes, we wanted things in our lives so badly, but we eventually realized they would never come to fruition.

That wasn't to say that Michael would never get married and have more kids. Not at all.

But there were no guarantees when it came to things like that.

When I thought about my own future, I remembered how I'd envisioned myself being married to Sergio now. I had imagined us starting our own life in Yerba. He would continue to work for the government, and on Sundays after church we would go to my parents' place to share a big meal where there would be love and laughter. We would take little trips whenever we could into the jungle to appreciate all the beautiful things that God had made. Fresh fruit would be abundant, along with fresh air.

All that had been turned upside down. I no longer had Sergio. My dad wasn't here. Yerba would never be the same again.

I didn't want to feel sorry for myself. I really didn't. But that didn't mean my heart didn't long for those days in the past.

As Chloe began talking about how much she loved to ride her bike, I turned my attention back to the girl.

I was so glad she had invited me to share this day with her.

But a world of danger awaited when I left this place, and I needed to prepare myself for whatever this day might hold.

CHAPTER FIFTEEN

MICHAEL and I met at the office and climbed into his mini-van. It was the perfect vehicle to use for stakeouts and surveillance because no one gave a second glance to the old silver vehicle with tinted windows.

Michael and I were going to sit and see if any deliveries were made to Marla today. If this stalker remained on schedule, there would be.

Perhaps the stalker knew that Marla was always gone on Fridays, that she spent all day at a local spa with her friends getting a massage, manicure, and drinking mimosas. Maybe he knew that every Saturday she had brunch with her friends. Apparently, those things had been her routine for the past five years.

"So how did Muffins with Mom go?" Michael asked, casually resting his hands on the wheel.

"I told you this before, but Chloe is just precious. It was fun."

"It wasn't weird?" He stole a glance at me.

"No, it wasn't weird. Not for me at least. And Chloe seems like she's comfortable with anything."

Michael smiled. "Yeah, it does seem like that, doesn't it? I have been blessed with a very easygoing child. For the most part, at least. I guess I need to wait until the teenage years before I can truly say if that's correct or not."

"That's probably true. But, really, she was great. She and I just chatted and ate muffins."

"What did you chat about?" He stole another glance at me.

I remembered the conversation I had with her, but I wasn't sure if I should share with Michael. Some things were best left unsaid. If someone had a secret, I was their girl. If there was one thing I could say about myself, it was that I wasn't a big mouth.

"Just girl stuff," I finally told him.

He raised an eyebrow as we parked across the street from Marla's house. "Just girl stuff?"

"I promise, if it was anything that you should be concerned about, I'd share. But there was nothing of importance—unless you think the fact that she wants a baby brother is important."

He let out a laugh. "She's always saying that. Unfortunately, that's not something I can deliver on right now."

"Maybe one day," I told him.

That distant look filled his gaze again. "Probably not. But I try not to tell her that."

I knew that Michael was convinced he'd never be able to find someone who would allow him to be a great dad and a great boyfriend at the same time. I had refuted his theory more than once, but I still didn't think he was convinced.

Instead of talking about it more, I glanced at Marla's house.

The place was lovely, and fit right into the whole Storm River façade. The two-story house had blue siding and cheerful shutters. A big porch wrapped around the front, and the yard was perfectly manicured. Houses just like it, except different colors, rose on either side.

"So this is where a watta botta motta lives . . . ?" I flinched. "Water botta model. No . . . water bottle motta. I can't say it!" I clamped a hand over my mouth. I hadn't even been trying to poke fun at Marla.

"Don't beat yourself up. It's a tongue twister." A deep chuckle escaped from Michael. "And, yes. This is where Marla Burns lives. I'm pretty sure she spent most of the money she made off her modeling days already, though. I think she's able to stay here because of Oscar."

My eyebrows shot up. "Do you really think he makes this much money?"

"He did with that one big case several years ago. Then

there's the movie and book deals. I think he's doing pretty well overall."

"You think he still loves her?" I wasn't sure where the question came from.

Michael shook his head. "No. Oscar mostly loves himself."

I didn't refute his statement. Instead, I leaned back in my seat, trying to settle in for a long day of doing surveillance. It wasn't my favorite thing, but it was a necessary evil.

"Any more revelations about the dead man from the lip-synching competition?" Michael asked.

"No." I suppressed a sigh. "I wish I did have some. But I still have no clue who that man was or why any of this is happening."

Tell him, an internal voice urged.

But my lips wouldn't move and refused to spill the truth about my father.

"I heard that organizers are trying to reschedule the lip-synching competition," Michael said.

I let out a groan. "I thought all my troubles had ended and that it was canceled. Well, not all of my troubles. But the superficial ones, at least."

At the mention of the competition, I remembered the Oleander Resort. I remembered the jump drive that had been hidden in my dad's things.

I'd slipped it into my pocket today, figuring it was safer to keep it with me than leave it at home.

I hoped I was right.

Michael grinned. "I think it's cute how antsy you were about the competition. Yet you didn't look foolish when we practiced. You did fine. Without you, we would have all been out of sync. You had us all arranged perfectly on the stage so the judges would never mark off for that."

"Exactly. I should be one of the ones directing instead of onstage."

Michael crossed his arms and looked back at the house again. "I wonder if this guy is going to show up today."

"We can only hope. With any luck, we'll be able to knock this out today and move on."

"I like the way you think."

As soon as the words left Michael's mouth, a car pulled up in front of Marla's house. It slowed and kept rolling by until it reached the corner, two houses down.

Michael and I glanced at each other.

That was weird. Why had someone slowed so early?

We watched from our position across the street as a man climbed from the vehicle with a box in his hands. He wore a uniform, like a delivery person might.

He bypassed the first house. Then he bypassed the second house.

Then he walked to . . . Marla's place.

Bingo!

"This just might be our guy," I muttered. Could it really be this easy?

"Or he's a private delivery driver with a really bad sense of direction," Michael said. "Let's not get too excited yet."

The man placed the box on Marla's front steps then glanced around.

That seemed suspicious within itself.

I had to resist the urge to jump out of the van and go question him right now.

But what if he truly was just a delivery driver? I couldn't act too early or I might blow our operation.

"What do you think?" I asked Michael.

"It's too soon. Let's be patient. And write down his license plate number so we can run it, just in case."

I did as he asked, and then we continued to observe the man. He glanced around again, as if to see if anybody was watching. Then he reached into his pocket and pulled out a paper. He placed it just inside the screen door.

"That's our guy." Michael reached for his door handle.

Just as we stepped onto the street, several bicycles sped past.

As they did, the man turned. He spotted Michael and me and took off toward his car.

If we didn't move quickly, we would be too late.

As the string of bikers stopped us in our tracks, the delivery man had just enough time to hop in his car.

"Back in the van!" Michael yelled.

Without wasting any more time, we jumped inside and Michael cranked the engine.

We waited until the bikers passed and then Michael pulled out.

But, by that time, the driver had already turned down another street.

Michael tried to catch up.

Just as we reached the next intersection, a woman wearing a fluorescent vest stepped out. She raised a sign in her hands, signaling for us to stop.

Michael pressed on the brakes and hit his palm against the steering wheel. "You've got to be kidding me!"

Another string of bikers zoomed past. As they did, the delivery driver's car disappeared down another street in the distance.

There was little hope we would catch up with him now.

Ten minutes later, we were still waiting for the last of the bikers to go past.

"He's gone," Michael muttered.

I would agree. "What now?"

"We go back and see what was on that paper." Michael turned around, and we headed to Marla's house.

We pulled up in front of her place and started toward the door. My steps faltered when I noticed that something had changed.

"The package is gone," I muttered.

Michael's eyes narrowed, and he shook his head. "And so is the note that had been left in the door. That guy must have circled back around and grabbed them."

That man was smarter than I'd assumed. I stared at the street, trying to picture everything playing out. "Do you think he had enough time to do that?"

Michael nodded, his neck still looking stiff. "I do. He realized he was caught and didn't want to leave any more evidence behind."

"Well, that stinks," I said, not sure what else I could say.

"Tell me about it." Michael rubbed his jaw, still looking annoyed. "We were so close."

"Yes, we were. I'm not even sure if he'll ever come back now."

"He knows we're onto him. We're going to have to think of another plan."

"Right now?" I asked.

"Right now, let's go back to the office and recalculate."

BACK AT THE OFFICE, while Michael worked out some details on the Burns case, I pulled out my phone and watched the security video footage I'd taken from the back-stage area at the Oleander Resort.

I had already watched it several times, but I kept hoping that something new would hit me.

The video quality wasn't great. I decided to stream it to my computer screen to make it larger. Maybe having that different vantage point would help me to see something I hadn't seen before.

Keeping the volume down so I wouldn't disturb Michael, I studied the images again.

I watched as Pinky walked to the door and propped it open, using a little doorstop.

I replayed it again.

It looked like Pinky was sweating. He'd said he was hot and that was why he'd opened the door.

But in this video, his motions looked jerky. Right after he opened the door, he glanced around, almost as if he was looking to see whether anybody was watching.

The motion was subtle, but it was there.

Doubt began to grow inside me.

I wasn't sure Pinky had told us the truth.

After all, he'd been sweating. He'd looked nervous. And he'd looked around to see if anybody was watching him.

Put them all together, and it wasn't exactly the picture of innocence.

As soon as Michael took a break, I called him over and told him about my observation, replaying the video as I did so.

"I think you're right," he muttered. "I'm surprised we never noticed that sooner."

"I think we were so busy watching everybody else in those frames, that we didn't pay enough attention to him."

"Do you want to go pay Pinky another visit?"

"If we don't have anything else to do, then yes."

And with that, we were out the door again.

CHAPTER SIXTEEN

IT TURNED out Pinky wasn't working at The Burger Joint today so we were going to have to wait to ask him those questions later. Instead, Michael and I went to the Oleander Resort.

It had been my idea. I wanted to see that exit door from the outside so I could get a better idea of exactly where the dead man had come in from. Would it give us answers?

I had no idea.

But it was worth a shot.

As we headed down the road, Velma called. "License plate on that car you saw today belongs to someone named Mary Lewis."

Michael frowned. "Did you find out anything else about her?"

"She's in her eighties, a retired schoolteacher, and widowed."

"Can you give her a call? See if she knows anything about Marla Burns?" Michael asked.

"I already did. She didn't answer. I called a neighbor also. Turns out Mary Lewis has taken a trip to Florida and isn't expected back until next month."

"Good to know." Michael glanced at me and shrugged. "Win some, lose some. We'll find this guy another way."

A few minutes later, we pulled up to the Oleander and climbed out. Michael and I walked around the building, trying to find the door that had been propped open before the murder. The place was bigger than one might think.

"Storm River reminds me of Disney World," Michael said, readjusting his baseball cap.

What in the world was he talking about?

"But there are no rides here," I said. "In my defense, I've never been to Disney. I've only seen pictures and heard about it."

"I'm not talking about the rides. I'm talking about all the resorts they have. I didn't realize it until just this moment. But even the names of some of the resorts here in Storm River remind me of Disney. Oleander, Founder's Circle, Waterside."

I didn't know if Disney would appreciate the comparison or not.

Based on what I knew, probably not.

Michael glanced at me as we paced the sidewalk along the perimeter of the massive building. "You've never been?"

"Never."

"You should go sometime. You would love it. Happiest place on earth."

"I'll keep that in mind." But in reality, I knew I wouldn't have cash for that for a long time.

I cleared my throat. "You know, there's one other thing we haven't considered about this case."

"What's that?"

"Mr. Harrington owns this place." He's one of the wealthiest men in town. With wealth comes power. Could he have anything to do with what happened?

"He'd never want negative publicity for his resort," Michael said.

"I can't argue with that." But the fact still bothered me. I needed to keep it in the back of my mind.

We reached an exit door nearest the backstage area, and I examined the outside of it. A small sidewalk led from an employee parking area at the back of the complex. Simple shrubs lined both sides of the area.

I stood there for a moment and glanced around.

To the right was the river area with all its boats and yachts. Beyond that was the golf course. To my left was another parking area reserved for guests of the resort.

This area where we stood right now was out of sight.

Someone could've easily parked back here without being seen.

However, the police hadn't found any stray vehicles in the lot. So how had the man gotten here? Had someone given him a ride?

If that was the case, then somebody else had to know about the man's presence here. It was likely they knew what he was going to do.

Or the man could have figured out another way here.

"What are you thinking?" Michael squinted against the sun as he stared at me.

"I'm trying to figure out how the man got here."

"And what are your theories?"

Was he testing me? Probably. I still had so much to learn.

"He could have driven and parked somewhere else and walked in," I started.

"Correct. That would mean his car is still out there somewhere."

"Someone could've dropped him off, which would mean he was working with somebody."

"Also true."

"He could have taken a taxi or an Uber."

"Hopefully, the police would have discovered that by now."

Or . . . "He could have come in via the river, by boat."

Michael's gaze met mine. "You really think he did that?"

I shrugged. "I'm just throwing out ideas. I'm trying to put myself in his shoes."

"You're trying to put yourself into the mind of someone who might be trying to kill you?"

I nodded. "I know it sounds weird, but a girl's got to do what a girl's got to do."

"Okay." Michael nodded slowly and stared off into the distance. "Even if that was true, how are we supposed to figure out which boat he came in on?"

"The marina manager keeps a log of that," someone said behind us.

I turned and saw the man who had worked with my father.

Dennis Haskell.

He wore a green uniform and held a bottle of water in one hand and some shears in the other.

My throat went dry.

Shears?

Did those fit the description of the murder weapon?

What had Hunter said? The murder weapon was a sharp pointy object that wasn't incredibly long. Shorter and thicker than a knife.

Like gardening shears maybe?

No, don't be silly, Elliot. Dennis is a perfectly nice man. Not a killer.

"Didn't mean to eavesdrop on you." Dennis shrugged. "I was walking this way when I saw you."

"No, that's very helpful," I told him. "Thank you."

"If someone was trying to hurt you . . . then the police need to figure out who that person was and why. That's what your dad would have wanted."

I appreciated Dennis's loyalty. I just hoped I could trust it. "I agree. My father was very protective."

"The marina manager's name is Harry. Tell him that Dennis sent you."

"We'll do that," Michael said. "Thank you for your help."

"One other thing," Dennis started to step away but paused. "There were two sets of footprints in the flower bed near that exit door."

I froze. "Really?"

He nodded. "That's right. I saw it myself. The police came and documented all of it, but last night's rain washed most of that evidence away."

"Did it look like two different men's footprints?" Michael asked.

"I'm no expert, but that would be my guess."

"Thank you." I reached into my pocket and handed him my business card. "And if you hear anything else . . ."

Dennis nodded. "I'll let you know."

"SO WHOSE NAME are you looking for?" Harry Liberman stared at a clipboard in his little dockside office as Michael and I stood there watching. The man appeared to be in his seventies, heavyset, and he dressed like a captain.

Michael had muttered something else about Disney again, but I didn't catch the reference.

Harry also spoke very slowly with long pauses between his words.

"We're looking for anybody out of the ordinary," Michael said. "We believe that the man who died at the resort this week may have taken a boat here. Have you already talked to the police?"

"I had one cop come over here looking at the boats. He talked to my assistant because I was in a meeting." Harry continued to study the clipboard, unfazed by the urgency in our voices.

I squeezed in closer, even though there was hardly any room inside the upscale shack. "Do you know what the assistant told this cop?"

"Can't say for sure. We have so many boats come and go around here. Especially this time of year." He stared at his clipboard a moment longer. "I'm not even sure exactly what I'm looking for. Out of the ordinary? Who's ordinary around here? Not most people I meet."

"Maybe you could look for anybody who maybe brought a boat in on Thursday and hasn't checked back in since then," Michael suggested.

"People can pay for different amounts of time that they

want to remain docked. Of course, we have our regulars." His voice still drew out every word.

"For the sake of brevity, let's just rule them out," Michael said, not appearing bothered by the way this guy drug his feet. "How about anybody else who has been docked here for the past three days whose name you don't recognize."

The man stared at the list. "I see two people that fit that description."

"Who?" I blurted.

The man clucked his tongue and shook his head. When he lowered his clipboard, I had to wonder if all of this had been for nothing.

"I'm not supposed to share that kind of information," he finally said. "Privacy and all."

We had to think of a way to get this information from him. This was our best lead yet.

"Dennis sent us over to talk to you," I reminded him. "And my dad used to work here. This is important."

The man's eyebrows raised. "Your dad?"

"His name was Eduardo, and he worked maintenance. Did you ever meet him?"

A grin spread across Harry's face. "Eduardo? Of course I did. He was a good man. I was really sorry about what happened to him. I don't know why God takes some people when they're way too young."

I didn't know the answer to that question either. I wished I did sometimes.

Instead of dwelling on it now, I waited to see if that new information would change Harry's mind.

He stared at his list again before letting out a long breath. "Listen, I can't tell you the names. It would get me fired if Mr. Birmingham found out about it."

Disappointment made my stomach plummet.

"But I can tell you what slips these boats are in. And if you happen to wander onto those boats and see some information . . ." Harry shrugged. "Then who am I that I'm supposed to recognize everybody who's out here?"

My spirits lifted. I liked the way this man thought. "That would be awesome."

He rattled off the numbers, and Michael and I walked toward the water.

Maybe we'd finally find some answers.

CHAPTER SEVENTEEN

THE FIRST BOAT that Michael and I came to was a million-dollar schooner. I couldn't exactly see that man who'd died taking a boat like this here.

For the sake of time, we decided to save that one for last.

Instead, we moved to the second boat, which seemed like a much more likely suspect.

The boat itself was still nice. I don't know enough about boats to identify exactly what kind it was. But Michael said something about it being a Boston Whaler. It could probably hold eight people, and there was a small cabin beneath the steering area.

Michael hopped on before taking my hand to help me aboard. The sun bore down on us as we paced the deck looking for any kind of clue as to this man's identity.

Since no wallet had been found on the man, had he left it inside the boat? Or had he set out with no ID on him at all?

I continued searching for any clues about this man's identity. I looked under seats, in containers, and in every compartment I could find.

I saw nothing.

"It looks clean," I told Michael. "Not one personalization in sight."

"There's only one place left to check—the cabin." Michael tried the door, but it was locked.

My chest deflated with disappointment. Had we come this far only to hit a river we couldn't cross? It was an old Yerbian expression, but it seemed appropriate now.

Before I could even ask, "what now?" Michael kicked the door.

With a crack, it opened.

My eyes widened.

I had to admit, I was impressed. I didn't know Michael could do that.

I glanced around, making sure nobody was watching. Thankfully, they weren't.

"Wait here," Michael said, his gaze making it clear he was dead serious.

I nodded. As he disappeared beneath the helm, I waited on deck, just like I'd promised.

My gaze scanned the marina, looking for any signs of trouble. There had to be at least twenty boats docked in this area. A few people lingered near their slips, washing their boats or lounging on their decks.

As I glanced back toward the marina manager's office, I spotted somebody duck behind the building.

It almost looked like the same man I had seen outside The Burger Joint yesterday, the one who'd tried to run us down.

Had he followed Michael and me here too?

The uneasy feeling in my gut grew. If he had, then we were probably looking at more trouble.

"Michael," I called down below. I glanced back in the direction where I'd seen the man. He appeared to be gone . . . but my gut told me he wasn't. "I think we have trouble up here."

As soon as I said those words, Michael was back on deck with me. "What's going on?"

"I saw somebody watching us from over there. I think it might be the same man we saw yesterday."

Michael's jaw tightened as he glanced in the direction I pointed. "I don't see him now."

"When I glanced up, he darted behind the building. Did you see anything down there?"

"I didn't have enough time to look. But we should probably get out of here before trouble comes our way."

Just as he said the words, a bullet sliced through the air.

Michael pushed me below deck. "Stay down!"

Someone was shooting at us? Someone really did want me dead, didn't they?

Another bullet flew through the air.

Wood splintered.

This guy wasn't backing off.

"What are we going to do?" The words rushed from my lips.

"We can't stay here." Michael's jaw flexed as his gaze swept the area. "We'll be sitting ducks."

I remained behind the door frame, my heart racing out of control. "But if we try to run, we'll be open targets."

"I know." Michael's face looked grim as he glanced back out the door. "Do me a favor. Look downstairs. See if you can find any keys."

"Keys?"

"Just do it."

Without wasting any more time, I sank into the cabin. The area was small, with barely enough room to move. There was a tiny kitchenette, as well as a small bed and desk.

Where did I start?

The desk, I realized. My hands trembled as I moved papers and logbooks and maps.

Nothing.

I went through drawers and looked in pencil holders.

Still nothing.

Maybe the keys had fallen.

On my hands and knees, I searched around the desk. It

was so dark and hard to see, though. Blindly, I reached forward, feeling for anything out of the ordinary.

Then my finger hit some metal.

I grabbed the small object, sight unseen, and pulled my hand back.

It wasn't a key. It was a . . . Yerbian flag?

What?

I couldn't think about it now. Instead, I kept feeling around, trying to find a key.

There was nothing.

Our one way of getting out of here had just fizzled.

What were we going to do now?

CHAPTER EIGHTEEN

I CLIMBED the steps toward Michael. "I can't find a key."

His face hardened. "Stay down there."

Just as he said the words, another bullet flew through the air, splintering the wall behind me.

Yelling sounded outside. I wanted to peek out and see what was going on. But I knew I couldn't take that risk.

A moment later, Michael ducked down beside me.

"What are we going to do?" I asked.

"Pray. And wait."

I could handle the praying part. The waiting part was much harder.

A few minutes later, I heard nothing but silence. No more bullets. No footsteps.

Nothing.

"Stay down while I check things out," Michael murmured.

Cautiously, he climbed toward the deck.

More people shouted in the distance. Something was happening up there.

At the top of the narrow stairway, Michael motioned for me to follow him.

I stepped onto the deck and froze.

In the distance, Bruno called for someone to stop.

The gunman made a run for it, though.

Bruno took off after him. Even I could tell from where I was that he wouldn't catch him. The man had too much of a head start.

But I was thankful that Michael and I were safe.

I glanced down at my hand and stared at the Yerbian flag there. It was a lapel pin, like the ones dignitaries often wore.

Someone associated with this boat was definitely connected to my time in Yerba. But how?

* * *

AFTER WE GAVE our statements to the police, Michael dropped me off at my car. He had to go pick up Chloe.

I'd be lying if I said I wasn't shaking. Yet again, my life felt like it was flashing before my eyes.

Why was someone doing this to me? I just couldn't figure it all out.

I sat in my car for a minute, but I wasn't quite ready to go home. I knew my mom was working and my sister was staying late after school again. I'd be returning to an empty house.

Instead, I decided to head down to one of my new favorite places. It was a restaurant called The Board Room, and it featured all kinds of board games that people could play while they ate from charcuterie boards.

The place was located on the water, just north of the nicer part of town. I wasn't sure if developers had planned it to be so rustic with the gravel parking lot and the boats docked out front. Either way, I liked it.

I wandered inside, found a table, and ordered a fruit and vegetable tray to munch on. Part of me was tempted to play a game of solitaire, but there wasn't time for that right now.

I had too many other things on my mind.

Instead, I pulled out my phone and did an internet search for the lip-synching competition. I knew people were video crazy in the world today, and I wondered if any of our competitors' videos—the ones who'd had a chance to perform—had been posted online somewhere.

A few minutes later, I got my answer. I found at least eight different videos that people from the audience had recorded and posted.

The first group, the lawyers, had done "Call Me Maybe." They were decent, but not winning material in my opinion.

Plus, their absolute lack of symmetry on stage drove me batty.

The second group, the car dealership, lip-synched to "Single Ladies." Again, they were okay, but nothing to write home about, as the saying went.

I went through the remaining videos also, looking for any familiar faces or anything that looked vaguely familiar.

Nothing caught my eye.

Until I watched the last video.

My eyes widened when I saw a familiar figure on the screen.

My landlord. Mr. Miller.

What was he doing at the competition? Was it a coincidence he'd been in the audience?

I didn't think so.

This was definitely going to be something I needed to think about.

After all, he had some type of prior connection to my father. Had the answer been in my face this whole time?

CHAPTER NINETEEN

I CONTINUED to munch on my tray and then I paid and left.
I felt slightly guilty for the indulgence, but coming here once
a week certainly couldn't hurt anything, could it?

As the darkness began to fall outside, I realized I really
should get home. Soon.

But first, I decided to meander down the docks and take a
moment to breathe the fresh air. There was always something about the water that made life seem just a little bit
simpler.

My dad had always said when life felt overwhelming, you
had to step back and try to look at the bigger picture. He'd
taken me out in nature to teach me life lessons that I still
carried with me today.

Being here right now. Smelling the musky scent of the
river. Hearing the water gently lap against the bulkhead.

Listening to my steps clack against the wood beneath me . . . It somehow made life more bearable.

"Fancy seeing you here again," someone said.

Without turning, I knew exactly who it was.

Hunter.

He docked a boat here he was working on in his free time.

I plastered on a smile as I turned to him.

"Hey there," I said. "I figured you would be working."

"I needed a little time to clear my head. Besides, it is my day off." He stepped out of the shadows, closer to me.

Just like the first time I'd seen him here, he was dressed more casually in cutoff jean shorts and a gray T-shirt. It was a nice look.

"I heard about the fiasco today down at Oleander." He paused in front of me, studying my face in the fading sunlight.

I felt my cheeks redden. Who would have thought a little bit of interfering could've led to so much trouble?

The look that Hunter gave me made it clear what he thought. This situation had him on edge.

"Crazy, huh?" It seemed a safe enough response.

He pressed his lips together before saying, "I'm glad nobody was hurt."

"Me too. I'm just disappointed that the guy got away."

"Someone obviously sees you as a target."

His words reminded me about my discovery today.

"Hunter . . . on that boat that was docked at the Oleander . . . I found a Yerbian flag."

His jaw tightened as he studied my face. "Did you?"

I nodded. "This just seems to confirm my fears. All of this somehow is connected with the political uprising in Yerba and whatever role my dad played in it all."

"I agree. We need to pinpoint more details."

I thought about that jump drive. Should I tell him about it?

My gut twisted. I wasn't sure.

So I decided not to. I wanted to keep that information to myself for a little longer.

Instead, I cleared my throat. "Speaking of everything that's been happening . . . is there any way the weapon used to kill that man backstage might have been . . . gardening shears?"

I almost hated to ask the question, especially since Dennis seemed like such a nice man.

"I suppose that's a possibility. Why?"

"I talked to one of the groundskeepers, and he was holding a pair. It just got me thinking . . ."

"I'll have my guys look into it." Hunter paused and studied my face. "I don't suppose you've had any revelations that you haven't told us about?"

"I haven't. I'm sorry. I'm just trying to keep my head above water."

"You've had a lot going on."

"I feel like I'm losing my mind just a little, like I'm caught on a hamster wheel that I can't get off of. Grief and danger seem to be right behind me, never letting up." I felt my cheeks blush and looked away. I hadn't intended to say that. "I'm sorry. I'm not sure why I told you that."

"I appreciate your honesty." He stared at me a moment before nodding and looking into the distance. "Look, I was just about to take my boat out for a little ride to help me clear my head. Want to come? It sounds like you could use some time away from all this craziness also."

I froze a moment, contemplating what I should say. Part of me wanted to jump in with an enthusiastic *yes*. The other part of me wondered if I could trust Hunter. He almost seemed too good to be true, and that fact alone made me feel cautious.

But the idea of getting out on the water was very tempting.

"Where are you headed?" I asked instead.

"I thought I'd head out toward the Potomac. Maybe see some of the lights from DC. They're pretty amazing."

It did have a certain allure. I hated going into the city, in general. But by boat? That sounded nice.

"Maybe I will," I finally said, reminding myself that I had to start taking some chances sometime.

A smile lit Hunter's face, and the expression—for a moment, at least—made it all feel worth it. "Great. I was just getting the boat ready to go when I saw you."

I prayed my excitement and decision to throw caution to the wind wasn't a huge mistake.

I STILL FELT UNUSUALLY nervous as I boarded Hunter's boat.

I wanted to blame it on the fact that I was so terrible when it came to dating. But this wasn't officially a date. Just because I found Hunter attractive and just because he invited me on his boat did not mean anything.

"Why don't you have a seat? Grab a water bottle from the cooler if you want while I get us out into the river."

I didn't argue. I grabbed a bottle of water before sitting on a bench right in front of the helm. I didn't try to fill the space up with meaningless talking. Instead, I let Hunter have all the time he needed to maneuver the boat out into the river.

The evening was going to be perfect for a boat ride. It was chilly, but I had a sweater on. The air felt crisp and clean. If I closed my eyes, I might imagine I was anywhere but here in Storm River.

For a moment, I pretended I was back in Yerba. On the Amazon. Listening to the macaws singing their songs. Watching monkeys swing from tree to tree. I even missed the sweltering air and the mosquitoes sometimes.

I hadn't admitted it, but I was homesick. There was no

doubt about it. How long would it take for this place to feel like my new home? What if it never did?

Finally, we got cruising at a steady clip. As we did, Hunter motioned for me to come stand beside him.

I joined him behind the wheel, and he pointed out various sites around the area. I had to admit that there was something about standing so close to him that took my breath away just a little.

I didn't like when people had this effect on me. I'd already had my heart broken once, and I wasn't in any hurry to jump back into that scene.

On the other hand, I knew I needed to simply turn my brain off and have some fun. I wasn't promising forever. I wasn't even promising one date. I was just trying to pretend to be a normal twenty-seven-year-old single girl who was hanging out with a friend.

A very handsome friend who just happened to be a detective.

That should make me feel better. Detectives were trustworthy, right?

Finally, Hunter navigated down another waterway, and I spotted lights on the horizon in the distance. He slowed the boat until we idled for a moment. Then he dropped the anchor and cut the motor.

He took my elbow, and led me to the bow.

The two of us stared at the city in the distance.

"That's the Washington Monument," I muttered. The tall

structure was lit up and looked majestic as it rose in the distance.

"It is."

"This vantage point is amazing."

"You should be here on the Fourth of July. The riverfront has the best view of the fireworks over our Capital." He raised his hand in the air, as if painting a picture for me.

"I bet it does." The wind swept through my hair, helping to soothe me. "Who would have thought a place full of so much corruption could look so beautiful."

Hunter glanced at me, his expression still reserved but friendly. "You don't like politics, I take it?"

"After I saw everything go down in Yerba, my perspective has been tainted," I told him. "I saw people put ideology over relationships. Goals over kindness. Politics over compassion. It was heartbreaking."

"I can imagine."

"I don't want to think that there are such bad people in the world." I shook my head. "Or maybe they're good people who've made bad choices. Maybe even bad people can seem good sometimes, for that matter."

"Or maybe people aren't all good or all bad. Maybe we're all a blend of the two."

"I suppose it's like the old saying: there are two dogs inside us. Whichever one we feed is the one that grows."

He nodded slowly as he stared ahead at the skyline. "Maybe. Which one are you?"

That felt like a loaded question. "I like to think I'm a good person who occasionally makes bad choices. But sometimes I don't know."

I remembered all the lying I'd done. Lying to my mom. Lying to people so I could get answers.

I definitely wasn't above any of these people I was speaking poorly of right now. I had so much to learn myself.

Hunter turned toward me, the moonlight hitting his face. His very symmetrical face. "Is that right? Because you seem like one of the most wholesome, kind-hearted people I've ever met."

Our gazes met, and I felt something pass between us. My heart rate kicked up.

What was happening right now?

As if in a dream, Hunter leaned toward me. "You're a fascinating woman, Elliot Ransom."

I licked my lips, my throat suddenly dry. "Am I?"

The air froze in my lungs. Was I about to take the plunge? Caution just needed to be flung . . .

He stepped closer. Caressed my jaw with the back of his fingers.

His eyes swept down from my eyes to my mouth.

Then our lips met.

Warmth oozed through my veins as Hunter reached for my waist, tugging me closer.

But, just as quickly as the kiss had started, Hunter pulled back.

A new emotion flashed on his face.

Was that . . . regret?

"Elliot . . . I'm sorry." His voice caught. "I shouldn't have done that."

I flinched.

Wait . . . Hunter was apologizing for kissing me?

I didn't even know what to think about that.

I only knew I wanted to get off this boat.

The sooner, the better.

CHAPTER TWENTY

HUNTER STEPPED AWAY and raked a hand through his hair. "I shouldn't have done that, Elliot."

I touched my lips, which were still warm and tingly from the kiss. "It's . . . okay."

It's okay? What else was I supposed to say? I hadn't exactly been in a situation like this before.

"I . . . didn't plan on that." Hunter paused a good four feet away from me and gripped the railing around the bow, almost as if he'd just been dealt a blow.

Distress, I realized. His body language showed major signs of distress.

All because of our kiss.

I froze, almost feeling like I'd been slapped.

"It's no big deal," I insisted, rubbing my burning throat. "Let's just forget it happened."

I'd never had to work so hard to make a guy feel better about kissing me. What was wrong with this picture?

So, so much . . .

Hunter swallowed so hard his neck strained with the action.

He stared off into the distance, at the lights of DC, as if gathering his thoughts . . . or thinking of more ways to make me feel humiliated.

Finally, he said, "I haven't dated since . . ."

He didn't have to finish his statement. I knew what he was trying to say.

He hadn't dated since his fiancée was murdered at the hands of a serial killer. The Beltway Killer. The man brought terror to women all over the DC area since he still hadn't been caught.

Hunter's ordeal would be enough to mess with anyone's mind.

"I get it, Hunter. Really. Don't beat yourself up." Even as I said the words, I made no effort to move from my spot. No, I was practically glued to the railing right now. If I moved any closer to him, only to have him draw back, I might be scarred for life.

Hunter finally looked over at me, his shoulders loosening ever so slightly. "You are one of a kind, Elliot Ransom. I try not to think about you. But I do."

At least there was that . . . compliment or insult? I wasn't sure still.

But I was entirely sure I was ready for this evening to be done. Coming on this boat ride had been a mistake.

"We should probably get back," I muttered.

Hunter stared at me another moment, his gaze full of distress, before nodding. "Right. Of course."

I released my breath when he went back to the helm and began steering us toward Storm River. It was a great excuse not to talk.

And that was just what I needed right now—silence so I could contend with my thoughts. So the breeze could calm me. So the scent of the water could offer me the comforts of home.

What I wouldn't do to go back in time. I'd had everything I wanted, I just didn't realize it. Now I had broken pieces of what had once been a beautiful life.

The quiet lasted for only a minute, however.

I looked up and saw a boat headed right toward us.

Hunter seemed to see the vessel at the same time.

"Hold on!" he yelled.

As the boat continued to charge us, I braced myself for the coming impact.

My entire body shifted as Hunter turned the boat.

I craned my neck, trying to see the oncoming vessel.

It still charged right toward us.

I pressed my eyes shut.

Please, Lord, help us. I'm sorry to cause such a fuss. Why do these things keep happening to me? Is there something you're trying to get me to see?

I waited, my fingers digging into the upholstered seat beneath me.

I tried to prepare myself for the impact, holding my breath in anticipation.

Nothing happened.

I heard waves lapping against the side of the boat. Felt myself shifting as the boat rocked. Heard Hunter muttering something into his phone.

Finally, I barely opened one eye.

The other boat sped away in the distance.

I released my breath and looked back at Hunter. "What happened?"

"He just barely missed us." Hunter shoved his phone back into his pocket, and then he looked back at me. "Are you okay?"

"Just shaken, but I'm okay."

"Good." His jaw tightened as he steered us back to the harbor area.

"You're not going to chase him?" I asked.

"He was driving a speedboat. There's no way I could catch up with him. But maybe one of the law enforcement vessels here on the river can. Besides, I reported the registration number. Maybe we'll get a hit."

What was going on here? Why was someone so determined to kill me?

Did I really want to know the answer to that question?

I WAS STILL REELING from everything that had happened. First, there was the ecstasy of being kissed. And then the total disappointment of hearing Hunter apologize for it. Then the terror of nearly being run down followed by the relief of realizing we were safe.

I had absolutely no idea what to think about everything. Maybe it was better if I didn't think about it at all. The last thing I needed right now was for my mind to be messed up with romance when I should just be focusing on other more important matters.

Hunter docked back in Storm River. Someone from the marine police came to take our statements and run the registration number.

Afterward, Hunter and I muttered a few awkward words to each other. Then I said good night, went back to my car, and drove home.

Who had tried to ram us? The men who wanted me dead, I supposed.

Then why had the boat pulled away at the last minute? They could have finished me off right then and there.

Once home, I chatted with my mom and sister for a few minutes. I didn't tell them everything that had happened. I couldn't bear to see the worry in my mom's gaze.

Then I went to my room and pulled out my dad's journal. I was anxious to read what he'd written, ready for a distraction from all my other thoughts.

I scanned the words on the page, trying to relish each one of them.

Toward the end of the entry, a name caught my eye.

Blaine Kingsley.

I sat up straight in my bed.

The man had been the US ambassador to Yerba, apparently.

My spine stiffened even more.

And my father had met with him after we moved to the States.

Suddenly, I knew exactly what my next step needed to be.

I needed to find this man.

Maybe he would have some of the answers that I was seeking.

CHAPTER TWENTY-ONE

BRIGHT and early the next morning, before going into the office, I stood in front of a stately home only about twenty minutes from downtown DC.

I'd found the address for Blaine Kingsley online, and I knew I wouldn't be able to concentrate on anything else until I had some answers. But I had to admit that I felt shaky as I stood outside his place right now, contemplating what exactly I was going to say to this man.

My general *modus operandi* was to wing it. But there were a lot of dangers in doing that, as Michael often reminded me. My instincts might be decent, but my experience was seriously lacking.

Come on, Elliot! You can do it. Take each challenge bit by bit. Waking, sleeping, walking too, there's nothing my girl that you can't do.

It almost sounded like a cheer. Not my intention. But maybe I needed a pep talk right now.

I dragged in a breath before walking up the sidewalk, climbing eight brick steps to the double front door, and ringing a doorbell that made it sound like a symphony had begun playing inside.

A moment later, a woman who appeared to be in her fifties, dressed in pearls and a blue sheath dress, answered with a proper, "Can I help you?"

I swallowed hard before starting. "Hi. I am trying to find Blaine Kingsley."

"Who's asking?" Her eyelids fluttered as she waited for my response.

Should I share my real name? Or use subterfuge?

This was the problem with winging it.

I rubbed my hands against my jeans. "I'm . . ."

"Elliot Ransom," a new voice said.

A man appeared from behind the woman. He had a tan complexion, a shock of dark hair, and a stocky build.

That had to be Blaine. But . . .

"You know me?" I squinted up at him as the sun hit the glass atop the door.

The man exchanged a look with the woman, and, after some silent communication, she disappeared into the house. He glanced around outside before motioning for me to follow him.

"Come sit in my study," he said. "I've been wondering if you would come."

A thousand questions rushed through my head. But all of them were overruled by the realization that I was finally getting closer to some answers.

Had it been wise for me to come into this place by myself without telling anyone where I was going?

I was about to find out.

Because I couldn't pass up this opportunity.

The inside of Blaine's house looked just as stately as the outside, with columns and a marble-like floor. The place smelled like lemon cleaner mixed with a cat hotel. It reminded me of the legislators' homes I'd visited in Yerba. Each of them had been trying to make a statement of their importance with their fancy furnishings. That had been my impression, at least. Blaine was no different.

We walked into an office to the right of the entry. High bookcases surrounded us on each side, and a massive desk sat in the center of the room atop an oriental rug.

"Can I get you some coffee?" Blaine asked, pausing near the door. "I have some I brought back from Yerba."

"I would love some," I said.

I could never resist Yerbian coffee. It was so much better than anything I'd found here—unless I included the coffee I'd gotten with Hunter a couple weeks ago.

But right now, I wanted to forget about all things Hunter.

Instead, I needed to turn my attention to all things related to my dad.

No distractions, I vowed. Now I needed to hold myself to it.

———

BLAINE REAPPEARED about five minutes later with a tray topped with two cups, some creamer, and various sweeteners. I went through the motions of preparing my coffee as I usually did. While I worked on that, Blaine shooed his cats from the room and closed the door.

Even coffee from my home country couldn't distract me now. I had too many other things on my mind. Too many unanswered questions. But it did taste wonderful.

Blaine took a seat behind his desk and stared at me. "I know you have a lot of questions for me, Elliot. I've been expecting you to show up. Why don't you go ahead and ask them?"

I liked the way he thought because I didn't want to waste any time either. I rested my coffee mug on my knee, one hand gripping the handle. "You knew my dad?"

He offered a curt nod. "I did. We met because of my work in Yerba. I was the ambassador to the country for ten years."

That confirmed what I already knew. Truth baseline established. Michael had taught me about that last week. "When did you move back?"

"I came back about six months ago when there were hints of the political uprising that was about to happen." His face remained placid, like a true diplomat's might.

I searched my mind, trying to come up with what I should even say next. I hardly knew where to start. There was so much on my mind.

Making a split-second decision, I found a photo of the dead man on my phone. I'd taken a screen shot from the security footage of the man's face when he slipped backstage. "Do you know who this is?"

He didn't even flinch as if surprised. Blaine really had been waiting for me to find him, hadn't he? He'd been anticipating all of this.

"I do," he said. "The man was a friend of your father's also."

My eyes widened. "What?"

I'd assumed that the man had come to kill me and that somebody had stopped him. What if I had it all wrong? What if he'd come to help me—or tell me something—and someone had stopped him?

Blaine took a long sip of his coffee. "It's true. His name is Alejandro Chavez. He worked with your dad in Yerba."

Alejandro Chavez? I'd never heard the name before, nor did it sound even vaguely familiar. "What was Alejandro doing here in Storm River?"

Blaine shrugged. "My best guess? He was here to keep an eye on you."

CHAPTER TWENTY-TWO

I SHOOK MY HEAD, trying to ignore the pounding that I was beginning to feel there. Nothing was making sense. That guy had been trying to help me? Like an undercover body-guard or something?

"I don't understand," I muttered.

Blaine let out a deep breath before taking another sip of his coffee, looking like he might be collecting his thoughts. "Your dad did not choose Storm River by accident. He chose Storm River because he believed there was somebody here who helped overthrow the Yerbian government.

"That's not right." My thoughts began to swirl. "My dad came here because my sister needed the lung transplant and because the government in our country was beginning to implode."

Blaine leaned closer, something sparking in his gaze. "Those were the main reasons Eduardo wanted to come here. But your dad was a very passionate man. And, once he started something, he didn't like to stop until he had what he needed."

I didn't like where this was going. My head pounded harder, and my thoughts swirled to a dizzying effect. "He was a spy, correct?"

Blaine stared at me for a moment before he said, "You figured that out."

"So he came here because there's some kind of connection between Storm River and Yerba?"

Blaine nodded again. "That's correct. He did not tell me all the details."

I ran a hand over my face, trying to force myself to comprehend all of this. "So, if the man who was killed was a friend of my father's, who killed him?"

He shrugged. "My guess is that it was somebody associated with the new regime that took power in Yerba."

Another bomb hit me. I hadn't expected any of this. In all of my theories and brainstorming, none of this had been on my radar.

"You're telling me that there are people who are a part of the new regime in Yerba who are here in the States right now?" I repeated for clarity. "If that's true, how did they get across the border?"

"They have their ways. And they're probably not people who look as you think they might look. They're people who blend in. Maybe they are even people who have been here for a while."

Was there a subtle warning in his voice?

I couldn't be sure, but a shiver went down my spine at his words. "I still don't know what this has to do with me or why someone would want to kill me."

Blaine leaned closer and lowered his voice. "Your father always saw something in you, Elliot. He saw a lot of himself. Although he wanted to protect you, another part of him wanted to develop those very qualities in you. He was very torn about his decisions."

It sounded like my father really had opened up to Blaine. I didn't know what to think about that.

I continued to think this through. "Do you know if this man who died—Alejandro—was just at the lip-synch competition to keep an eye on me?"

Blaine shifted before shaking his head. "I don't know."

"Is there anything else you can tell me?"

He shrugged. "Anything else you're going to have to figure out for yourself, Elliot. I'm afraid I've already told you too much. I will say this—you need to be careful because there are dangerous men at play here. Keep a low profile, and always watch your back."

I HADN'T BEEN able to get anything else out of Blaine. But at least I'd learned what I did.

I decided to head to the office. But, as I stepped outside, that feeling hit me again.

The feeling of being watched.

The hairs on my neck seemed to rise.

I paused on the sidewalk and glanced around. I saw only the expected. Cars parked on the street. A couple walking their dog. A family strolling together around the corner.

No one who looked vicious. Or obvious. Or dangerous.

But I couldn't forget Blaine's words. *Dangerous men at play here. Keep a low profile, and always watch your back.*

As I reached my car, I saw a paper on the windshield.

I closed my eyes. Not a note. They were never a good sign. You didn't have to be a super sleuth spy to know that.

Carefully, I pulled it from under my windshield wiper.

I blanched at the words written there.

You have something we want.

My throat went dry.

I glanced around. Someone had known I was here.

Were they still watching me?

As I saw a police car patrol past, I realized the person who'd left this was probably long gone. There were certain perks to living in an upper-class neighborhood, I supposed.

I stared at the words again. *You have something we want.*

The jump drive.

It was the only thing that made sense.

Right now, it was tucked snuggly in my pocket.

That's where it would stay. Someone would only take it over my dead body.

CHAPTER TWENTY-THREE

AS I DROVE toward the office, my phone rang. When I saw it was my mom, I put it on speaker, wondering if she was calling about my sister.

Was Ruth sick? Or had she caught a ride with another bad driver?

"Good morning," I said, trying to sound perky.

"Elliot Ransom, are you working for a private investigator?" Her voice rose, just below a yell—which she never did unless she was *really* angry.

I felt my insides tighten faster than a jaguar pouncing on prey. "What?"

"Don't *what* me, Elliot Ransom. You haven't been telling me the truth."

I couldn't have this conversation while I was driving. I

pulled to the side of the road. Just when I thought things couldn't get worse.

"Mama . . ."

"Go ahead. Explain. Tell me I'm wrong. But I know I'm not."

"Why do you think that?" I asked, rubbing my temples.

"I saw the article in the paper this morning," she told me. "It was about that man who died. And it mentioned the lip-synching competition and the teams who were there. It clearly listed Driscoll and Associates Private Investigative Firm. Elliot . . ." Disappointment rang through her voice.

"Mama . . ." I'd take anger over disappointment any day.

"Then it's true?"

I nibbled on my lip for a moment. I couldn't lie to her anymore. "It is. I just didn't want you to worry. You already have so much on your shoulders."

"That's no excuse for lying. I taught you better than that."

"I know, but . . . I just didn't correct your assumption." I knew my words sounded weak and unconvincing.

"That's the lie of omission!"

"Okay, you're right. I don't know what to say." I squeezed my eyes shut.

My mom remained quiet a moment. "I'm so disappointed in you, Elliot. I might expect this from your sister, but never from you."

Her words felt like a slap in the face. I deserved them. But that didn't mean I liked them. "I didn't mean to upset you. I wanted to protect you."

"What about this dead man?"

Should I tell her the truth about that also? Maybe. But the words wouldn't leave my lips. How much more could she handle right now?

"I was in the wrong place at the wrong time," I said instead.

"We'll talk more later. Right now, I've got to get back to work. But this isn't over."

"I know, Mama."

Without saying anything else, she ended the call.

I closed my eyes and leaned my head against my seat.

My gut told me this wasn't going to be a good day. Not by any stretch of the imagination.

Yet, at the same time, how could it get much worse?

I KEPT one eye on my rearview mirror as I headed down the road. Someone had known I went to Blaine's house. That same person could very well be following me now.

The realization made all my muscles stiff and ready to react.

There was something else that I knew I needed to do. As much as I might want to keep certain information to myself, that would not be beneficial to this investigation. Plus, could I be arrested for withholding evidence?

I didn't know. And it didn't matter. I knew my conscience would not let me rest until I told Hunter that I had learned this man's identity.

I put my phone on speaker and called him. He answered on the first ring.

As soon as I heard his voice, my stomach squeezed. Memories of our time on the boat last night filled me. That was the last thing I wanted to think about right now.

"Hunter, it's Elliot," I started, my voice sounding stiffer than I would like.

His voice seemed to soften. "Hey, Elliot. Good to hear from you."

Before he could say anything personal, which I wasn't sure he was going to do, I rushed in with what I had to tell him. "I know the name of our dead man."

"What?"

"It's a long story," I started.

"I have time."

"It turns out there's a former ambassador to Yerba named Blaine Kingsley who lives in Storm River and he knew my father. I paid him a visit this morning and showed him a picture of our dead man. He recognized him. Gave me a name even."

"What's his name?"

"Alejandro Chavez."

"What else did he say?"

"That a member of the regime that came into power in Yerba may have killed our victim, who was a friend of my father and probably watching out for me."

Hunter was quiet a moment before it sounded like he clucked his tongue. "I'm going to need this ambassador's name and number so I can talk to him myself."

"I don't have his number, but his name is Blaine Kingsley." I rattled off his address.

"I'll see what else I can find out. Thank you for sharing the information with me."

"It's no problem. Glad I could help."

Hunter cleared his throat. "Since I have you on the phone, I thought I'd let you know that the boat that tried to hit us last night was stolen."

I frowned. "Why is that not surprising? I assume that means there are no leads as to who was behind the wheel?"

"Not yet. But we're still working on it."

"Good to know."

"Elliot, about last night . . ." Hunter's voice trailed, almost as if he didn't know what to say.

"You don't have to talk about it," I rushed, perfectly happy to avoid the subject. "I'm good."

Hunter let out a little sigh. "I wish things weren't so complicated."

"I know what that's like. I really do. Let's just forget it happened." I'd be content to forget this conversation as well.

"That's going to be easier said than done."

Hunter's words caused heat to rise on my cheeks. So maybe the kiss hadn't been completely terrible for him.

"We can talk later, okay?" I finally rushed, anxious to get off the phone.

"Okay. I'll be in touch. Be safe, Elliot."

"You too." As I ended the call, I glanced in my rearview mirror again. I didn't see anyone following me.

But the bad feeling remained in my gut.

CHAPTER TWENTY-FOUR

FINALLY, I got to the office. It felt like an entire week had passed in only a day.

I glanced at the time. It was only ten o'clock.

Not even a day. Or a half day.

Even though it was Saturday, Oscar asked the team to work a couple Saturdays each month, depending on our caseload.

Michael was already there, and he had Chloe with him. Velma sat on the floor with her, trying to build a tower out of some paper cups. Oleander was written on the side of each of them.

Velma must have taken them from the competition. It wasn't a surprise. I'd even seen her sneaking out with some leftover toilet paper from our restroom here at the office once.

"Elliot! Elliot! Elliot!" Chloe jumped to her feet and threw her arms around me. "I was hoping I'd see you."

I rubbed the girl's back as I pulled her into a gentle hug. "It's great to see you too. You came to work with your dad today, huh?"

"For a little while. We're going to my soccer game later, but dad said he had a little work to do first."

I glanced at Michael. He stood in the doorway that separated our offices from Velma's reception area. His hands were stuffed into his pockets, and he smiled at Chloe. It was the smile he reserved just for his daughter, one full of affection, admiration, and attachment.

Any female would be honored to receive a smile like that.

"Chloe, let go of Elliot for one minute. I need to talk to her in the office, okay?"

Chloe released me. "Okay, Daddy!"

She joined Velma on the floor again, where they began to build their tower of cups.

I slipped into the office and closed the door behind me, waiting for what Michael might have to say. The way my day was going, it would be more bad news.

Part of me wanted to pour out to him everything I had just learned. The other part of me wondered how wise that would be. I hated feeling so torn. But I did.

I sat in my office chair and twirled around to face him, waiting for whatever he wanted to say. I had to admit that I felt a little sick to my stomach.

"I couldn't sleep last night," he started. "So I made a list of everybody who was backstage at the time of the lip-synching competition."

My heart raced for a moment. This conversation wasn't going in the direction I anticipated, but I was fine with that. "Okay . . ."

"Unfortunately, I couldn't find anybody who seems to have a connection with you or your father." Michael frowned.

My hopes sank. "That's too bad."

"I was also able to get up with the guy from The Burger Joint this morning. It turns out, that man who ended up dead paid Pinky twenty dollars to prop open the door."

My breath caught. So the burger guy had been lying. If he lied about that, what else had he not told all the truth about?

"Do you think there was more to it?" I asked.

"I'm not sure yet. Pinky seemed super nervous as he confessed. He said it hadn't seemed like a big deal at the time, that he never thought that man would end up dead."

I nodded my head slowly. "At least we're getting more information. The key is figuring out if it's leading anywhere."

"Exactly," Michael studied me for a minute. "How about you? Anything new?"

I remembered my visit with Blaine today. The threat left on my car. The boat that tried to hit Hunter and me. And, last, but not least, my mother discovering what I really did for a living.

How much could I share with Michael without giving away too much information?

I wasn't sure. But it was clear that he deserved to know at least something. I prayed I didn't regret sharing.

"I learned the name of the dead man," I finally admitted.

Michael's eyes widened. "That's great. What is it?"

"It's Alejandro Chavez. Apparently, he knew my father."

Michael shook his head, a little too quickly. "What?"

I knew I wasn't making much sense. There was so much to explain. So much to still keep secret.

"I managed to track down a diplomat who used to be in Yerba, and he identified our victim."

"So it sounds like that man may have been there to help you, and somebody else killed him?" Michael stared at me, as if trying to process that twist.

"That's my understanding."

He took his hat off, raking a hand through his thick, dark hair. "Man. There's just so much about this that doesn't make sense."

"I agree."

"The more I learn, the less I like it."

"Me too," I said.

A few minutes of silence fell, and I could tell Michael was processing what I'd told him. After a moment, he shook his head again.

"As much as I'd love to stay and talk about this more, I've got to get Chloe to her soccer game," Michael finally said.

"But I know that Oscar wants us to stake out Marla's house again a little bit later—while Marla is gone. I was hoping to swing by after the game and then maybe we could do that."

"That's fine."

"We'll talk more when I get back. Maybe you can research this guy more while I'm gone, now that you know his real identity."

"I think I will do that. Good idea."

He stared at me a moment longer before nodding. "I'll meet you back here in a couple hours, and we'll go from there."

"Sounds like a plan."

CHAPTER TWENTY-FIVE

AFTER MICHAEL AND CHLOE LEFT, I quietly sat in my office for a moment, trying to reflect on everything I'd learned so far.

I still had that jump drive in my pocket. I needed to decide if I wanted Michael's friend to try and unlock it or not. Part of me didn't want to let it out of my sight. But, if I didn't, would I ever know what was on it?

Was there information there worth killing for?

I remembered Palmer saying that someone had broken into his office shortly after that bag of my dad's belongings had been retrieved. Had someone been looking for the jump drive?

Maybe the person looking for it didn't know it had been in the safe at the resort this whole time.

I did a quick internet search on Alejandro Chavez, but I found no mention of him online.

Of course.

If he were smart, he would have steered clear of leaving any kind of digital footprint. My bet was that, if I wanted information on him, most of it would be classified.

There was only one person I could think of that I needed to talk to right now.

My landlord.

He had been in the audience on one of those videos of the lip-synching competition, and I wanted to know why. Plus, I hadn't paid much attention when we moved here, but my dad had somehow known this man before we came. What if Mr. Miller also had some kind of connection to our family that we hadn't realized yet?

After I found his address, I took off toward his place. Fifteen minutes later, I pulled up to one of the newer homes here in Storm River.

It was built to look like an older style craftsman, but everything about it was actually new. I especially liked the clean white siding and the big front porch.

I didn't even have to knock on the front door at his place. As soon as I climbed out of my car, Mr. Miller walked around from the backyard pushing a lawnmower.

His eyes lit with recognition when he saw me.

"Elliot." He abandoned his mower and stepped toward

me. "What brings you by this way? Is everything okay at the house?"

"Everything is fine. I'm sorry to drop by unannounced."

Mr. Miller stopped in front of me. "What's going on?"

"How did you know my father?" I cut right to the chase, knowing I didn't have any time to waste.

Hey, I'd nearly rhymed, and I hadn't even been trying.

I gave myself a mental pat on the back.

Mr. Miller's face turned stoic. "I didn't directly know your father. But we had mutual friends in this area, and I heard he was looking for a place to live."

I eyed the man, looking for any signs of deceit. His gaze appeared steady. He wasn't sweating or fidgety. Was he actually telling the truth?

Or was he the master of being deceitful? Any spy—or anyone who worked with spies—would be, right?

"Mutual friends?" I repeated.

He shrugged, like it wasn't a big deal. "I worked with a man who used to live in Yerba. This man passed along my name to your father. End of story."

Maybe that was just the information I was looking for. "Who is that man?"

"His name was James Johnson. Unfortunately, he passed away a few months ago in a car accident."

Another person connected to my father had died? I stored that information away, just in case it ever became useful.

"So you had never met my father until we moved here?" I repeated, making sure I was understanding this. *If in doubt, reframe the same question in a different way.* Another one of Michael's tips.

"That's right. Why are you asking?" His hands went to his hips as he waited for my response.

"Because you were at the lip-synching competition on Wednesday evening, and I got curious why."

He shrugged, his shoulders looking stiff. "I was. Is that a problem?"

Either Mr. Miller was a good actor, or he was telling the truth right now. Because he seemed really clueless about this conversation.

"Did you know the man who died that day?" I pulled out my phone and held up his picture.

He studied it for just a minute before squeezing his eyes shut and looking away. "No. I didn't, God rest his soul. I still don't understand why you're asking these questions."

"This man who died had some connection to me, and so do you. You just happened to be at the lip-synching competition, so . . ."

He let out a low groan and took a step back, raising a hand in the air. "I didn't have anything to do with that."

"Then why were you at the competition?" I repeated.

"One of my coworker's sons was competing. He was a part of the troop that did 'Single Ladies.'"

I'd never get the image of those men doing that song out of my head.

"Plus, I like to play tennis there sometimes with some friends," he continued.

So Mr. Miller was on Team Oleander. I made a mental note.

"When did you get to the competition that evening?"

"I got to the Oleander before it started, and I didn't leave until the police released us."

"Did you get up at all? To go to the bathroom or anything?"

"I didn't." His gaze darkened. "And I'm starting to not appreciate all your questions."

I pretended like I didn't hear him. "Did you go with anyone who can verify that information?"

"I'm sure my wife will tell you the same." He paused and stared at me, his eyes narrowing with disbelief. "You think I might have killed this man?"

I remembered all that diplomacy my father had. The way he was able to put people at ease instead of on edge. I really need to learn some of that right now.

"No, I don't think that. I was hoping that maybe you saw something, though. Maybe someone who's connected to my father."

"If I remember correctly, your father worked at that resort, right? That means he could've had all kinds of connections to the people there."

I couldn't argue with what the man was saying.

"Theresa," he called to a woman who stepped out from the backyard with a rake in her hands. "This is one of my tenants, Elliot. She's asking about that lip-synching competition. I sat beside you the whole time, right?"

The woman, a blonde with curly hair piled high on top of her head, stepped toward us. "Yes, that's right. I was actually surprised because Roger always has to go to the bathroom lately. We can't even take a two-hour road trip without having to stop twice."

Mr. Miller shrugged. "What can I say? I was having a good evening on Wednesday. Now, any more questions?"

I shook my head. "No, thank you so much for all your help. I really appreciate it."

As I climbed back into my car, I realized there were certain people I could rule out. Mr. Miller, for starters. But was anybody really rising to the forefront as my lead suspect?

I pulled my seatbelt on. No, they weren't.

And that was too bad.

I SAT in my office and tried to sort out my different ideas for various suspects.

I felt fairly confident I could eliminate Pinky, the burger guy. He'd only opened the door for the money.

Mr. Miller was on my list also, but it appeared he had an

alibi to verify he was in the audience during the time of the murder.

And then I had . . . no one else.

I leaned back in my chair and let out a sigh. That was not the conclusion I wanted to draw.

But maybe I did have one question answered. I had felt like I had been being followed for the past several weeks. Was it possible that this Alejandro guy had been the one tailing me? Had he simply been watching out for me?

Or was there an entirely different set of people in play here, people who were watching me because of my relationship with my dad?

And why exactly had my dad come here to Storm River? What had he known that I didn't?

I had so many questions and so few answers. All of them circled in my head like Andean condors looking for their lunch.

Finally, Michael and Chloe returned.

I forced myself to smile as Chloe skipped up to me with a grin on her face.

"How was your game?" I asked.

"We won again." She raised her arm in victory.

I gave her a high five as she stood in front of me, some kind of gooey red syrup stuck around her lips.

"Snow cone," Michael explained, stopping beside us. "It's our victory treat when we win."

"I'm surprised I don't see a little red mustache on you too," I told him, keeping my expression innocent.

"Not this time. Don't worry. When I have one, I wear it like a badge of honor."

I didn't doubt his words.

Michael swung his keys around his fingers and turned toward me. "You ready to go?"

"Sure thing." I plucked my purse from the floor and followed after them. We waved goodbye to Velma, knowing we probably wouldn't be back here today.

I wondered if Chloe was going to come with us on a stakeout. She'd never come along with us on any of our cases before. But I wasn't sure if Michael had a backup sitter or not.

"Chloe's going to have a play date for a few hours at one of her friend's houses," Michael explained, almost as if reading my mind. "Her friend doesn't live too far away from Marla, so I hope you don't mind if we take a quick detour first."

"Not a problem at all," I told him.

We headed toward Marla's house. As we did, Chloe pulled out a long pink ribbon and began to work on getting the knots out of it. She wasn't having any luck.

"Here, let me try," I offered.

She handed it to me, and I began to work on it. This was going to take a while. These knots were tight.

Chloe pointed at the mega church as we passed. "Look, it's Grandma and Grandpa."

I glanced around, but I didn't see anybody walking outside the building. "Where?"

She pointed again. "On the sign."

I lifted my gaze and saw the smiling couple on the church's billboard. I sucked in a quick breath as the truth hit me.

Had I just heard Chloe correctly?

"Wait . . . those people in the picture are your grandma and grandpa?" I asked, making sure I wasn't jumping to conclusions here. But the pastor's name *was* Mike. Was Michael actually Michael Jr.?

"Yeah," Chloe said. "My dad didn't tell you?"

My gaze went to Michael, who stared straight ahead at the road as if that might make him immune to this conversation. Finally, he looked over and shrugged, a sheepish grin on his face.

"They're your parents?" I continued.

"I told you it was complicated," he finally said.

I tried to remember what I had said about mega churches the first time we'd passed this place, and I hoped I hadn't said anything too offensive.

"My grandma's speaking at a conference this week," Chloe continued. "That's why she couldn't come to Muffins with Mom. And Granddad is on a personal retreat to plan his sermons."

"That sounds nice."

"He sent me a picture of the cabin where he's staying in the mountains. It has a swimming pool *inside*." Her voice lifted in awe. "It looks like *so* much fun."

"A swimming pool? Inside? That does sound nice."

And expensive. I didn't say that out loud. I already sounded judge-y enough.

"My grandma's been speaking a lot more lately," Chloe continued. "I think she really likes it."

I was pretty sure the girl never ran out of things to talk about. Maybe she got that from her grandma. It definitely hadn't been from Michael.

"Well, it's always good to find something that you like," I told her.

"Dad and I are going to go to church there tomorrow. Aren't we, Dad?"

Michael's gaze darkened. "I think we're going to go to our other church tomorrow since Grandma and Grandpa are out of town. We talked about this. Remember?"

Just then he pulled up at a little house. Almost before he put the van in Park, Chloe had opened the door. Great timing on his end.

"How about if I give this ribbon to your dad after I get the knots out?" I called.

"Sounds good!" She hopped out, heading toward the sidewalk.

As she did, I put the ribbon in my pocket. I'd work on it later.

"Chloe, wait for me," Michael called.

He rushed from the van and walked her to the door.

Her friend's mom opened the door with a wide grin and ushered Chloe inside. Michael said a few words to her before the woman glanced at me and waved.

Then Michael was in the minivan again.

I contemplated exactly what question to ask him first.

Because I had so, so many.

CHAPTER TWENTY-SIX

I DECIDED to wait until we were at Marla's house, watching for her stalker to appear, before asking Michael any questions. That way there wouldn't be any interruptions.

As he put his van into Park two blocks over, I expected to settle back and wait. Instead, Michael opened his door. "The minivan has been compromised. We're going to need to set up surveillance somewhere else."

"Sure thing." It made sense.

I followed him as we cut between some houses until we finally stopped behind Marla's place.

"If we stand over here, we'll have a good view of anyone who pulls up," Michael said.

I glanced at the sheets that Marla had hanging up back here. They'd make a nice cover. We stood near the fence, our bodies concealed, and we began our wait.

As we did, I glanced at my partner-in-crime-solving.

"I hope I didn't say anything insulting about your parents before I knew they were your parents," I started.

I needed to get that off my chest first. It was bad enough that my mom was mad at me. I didn't need to anger everyone who was close to me.

"You didn't," Michael said.

"I had no idea . . ."

His jaw stiffened, and he stared out at the street, a certain edginess coming over him. "I don't want to talk about it."

I could tell this was a sensitive subject and that I would have to proceed with caution. Maybe I should just stop here, but I knew I wouldn't be able to do that.

"How long have they been at the church?" I asked finally.

"Twenty years."

"So you grew up at that church then . . ." Things began to click in place in my head, a better mental picture of Michael's upbringing.

"That's right. I was a preacher's kid in town."

I could only imagine what that was like. It was hard enough at a small church, I would imagine. But in a big church where the preacher and his wife could practically be like celebrities?

You'd be in the spotlight . . . or the fishbowl, if that's what you wanted to call it. It had to be a lot of pressure, especially in a town like this that was all about image.

I wanted to ask more questions. I really did. But I had a feeling I shouldn't push anymore for now.

There was a story there. I didn't know what it was, but I hoped Michael might share it with me when he wanted to.

Michael glanced over at me. "Find out anything new about the case involving our dead guy?"

I got the hint. He wanted to move on.

"I tried to brainstorm some ideas and suspects, but I wasn't very successful."

"Let's keep digging. We'll come up with something sometime."

"I can only hope."

We sat there for a few minutes in silence. As we did, my mind went back to last night. To being on the boat with Hunter. What I wouldn't do right now for a good girlfriend to talk things over with. My mind had been messed up ever since I'd felt that man's lips touch mine.

Actually, before that.

Sergio had broken my heart, and I hadn't been interested in dating since then. But there was something different about Hunter. He almost made me want to give dating a chance.

At least, he had before last night.

"What are you thinking about?" Michael narrowed his eyes as he studied my face.

"Do you really want to know?" I glanced at him and saw that he looked sincere enough.

"I wouldn't have asked otherwise."

"I'm thinking about last night, if you really want to know." I frowned, my lips tingling again as I thought about that kiss of doom.

"What happened last night?" He sat up a little more.

"I was down at The Board Room then I ran into Detective Hunter."

He raised his eyebrows. "Is that right? That's not where I expected this story to go, but okay . . ."

"And he invited me to go out for a boat ride with him."

Michael's eyebrows climbed higher. "And did you?"

"I did."

He crossed his arms, settling in for the story. "And how was it?"

How much did I say? I desperately wanted someone to talk this through with. "It was . . . nice. I had a good time talking to Hunter outside of all this investigative stuff where we usually interact."

That was safe enough. That was me. Play-It-Safe Elliot.

"Do you like him, Elliot?" Michael sounded like he really wanted to know.

His question surprised me, and, this time, my eyebrows shot up. "I'm . . . I don't know. I don't know him enough to say, I guess."

"Okay . . . was it a date then?"

"No. Definitely not."

He waited. The silence seemed to beg for details.

The pressure squeezed in on me until I finally blurted, "He kissed me."

Michael shook his head and raised his hand. "What? Oh no. We can talk about a lot of things. But anything girly like PMS or things like that . . . I can't listen to. And that includes details about your dates."

"Well, like I said, it wasn't a date."

Michael dropped his head to the side. "He kissed you. I would call that a date. And like I said, I don't really want to talk about this. Your love life is your love life."

But I hadn't even told him the worst part yet.

"He kissed me and then apologized," I announced. It was like the thoughts couldn't stay contained inside my head and were desperate for an escape.

Michael shook his head again, almost like he'd come up out of the water and needed to shake off. "What?"

"It's true." My cheeks warmed at the humiliation of it all. "What does that even mean? That he regretted doing it?"

"That's a question you would need to ask him, Elliot."

I let out a long breath. I'd been hoping for too much when I thought all guys might universally share one mind and Michael might tell me what that said mind was thinking.

"I know, I know," I said. "It just doesn't make sense to me. And, in case I haven't ever mentioned this before, I'm really no good at this dating thing."

"You have mentioned that before." Michael stared off into the distance a moment before shaking his head again. "He apologized? You should never apologize for kissing a pretty girl."

"Is that right?" And did that mean that Michael thought I was pretty? Not that it mattered. But part of me delighted in that fact.

"Sorry." Michael's gaze flickered up to mine. "I broke my own rule. No more talking about this. But what about Jono? I thought the two of you were dating."

"Jono? I already explained that situation to you." I'd only gone out with the rich playboy because I thought he might know my father, but he'd given no indication that he did.

"You explained, but you said you might go to a golf tournament with him."

"That's still a couple weeks away, and I didn't give a definitive answer."

Before I could say anything else, I spotted somebody walking toward Marla's house.

I nudged Michael. "Is that our guy?"

Michael perked up as he looked away from me, no doubt relieved for the excuse to end this conversation.

"I think it might be," he muttered. "Let's get ready. We can't let him get away this time."

MY LEGS BURNED as I ran from behind the house.

"Hey!" Michael yelled.

The man paused on the sidewalk.

It was definitely the same guy.

When he saw us, he took off in a run. But there was no way he would get to his car in time.

He seemed to realize that also and rushed down the sidewalk instead.

Thankfully, Michael was fast. Much faster than I was.

He caught the guy in fifteen seconds flat, tackling him on someone's lawn.

As he did, something fell from the man's hands.

A heart that said, "You're Mine." The piece was broken in half.

I shuddered.

"I didn't do anything!" he yelled. "I'm calling the police."

"You didn't do anything?" Michael growled. "Then why are you stalking Marla Burns?"

"Stalking? I don't know what you're talking about."

I paused beside them, sucking in deep breaths and making another vow to start exercising soon. "We know you've been leaving those threats for her."

"Threats?" He sat up, his face flushed and his eyes narrowed. "I would never threaten Marla."

Michael pulled the man to his feet. "Then you have some explaining to do."

He raised his hands. "Okay, okay. Whatever you need to know. Just don't hurt me."

"We're not going to hurt you," Michael muttered. "Who are you?"

"My name is AJ Lewis."

"And how do you know Ms. Burns?"

"I saw her in a coffeeshop a few weeks ago, but I was afraid to talk to her. She was the most beautiful woman I'd ever seen, especially when she took a sip of her coffee . . ." The man's face got a far-off look, as if he was picturing it in his head.

"Then what are you doing at her house?" Michael continued.

"I'm trying to let her know how much I care about her."

"By sending her dead flowers?" I asked.

He blanched. "Dead flowers? I would never do that. They were alive when I left them."

"How hot was it that day?" Michael's eyes narrowed with thought.

"It was a scorcher. It climbed into the upper eighties. Unseasonably warm."

The sun must have wilted them, I realized.

"What about the poisoned chocolates?" I asked.

"Poisoned chocolates? Never. But I left those on another hot day."

So the chocolates had melted. We'd never had them tested because Marla had tossed them.

"What about the note saying you had your eye on her?" Michael continued.

"I was just trying to be sweet, not creepy." He shrugged. "I don't understand."

"What about that broken heart?" I pointed to the shattered words on the ground.

"It broke when you guys tackled me!"

I supposed that made sense. But . . .

"You ran back and took the package and note on that day we chased you," I said. "Why? Those aren't the actions of an innocent man."

"I thought you were package thieves." AJ shrugged. "What else was I supposed to think?"

Michael let out a long sigh and ran a hand over his face. "Marla thought you were threatening her. She hired us to make sure she was safe."

"I would never want to hurt her. I just wanted to get her attention."

"You got her attention all right," I muttered.

"Are you guys arresting me?" AJ asked, his voice becoming more high-pitched with every word.

Michael shook his head. "No, not arresting you. But we do need to have a talk about how to win a woman over . . ."

I wondered exactly what Michael might say.

One thing was for sure: this case hadn't turned out the way I expected.

CHAPTER TWENTY-SEVEN

WE DECIDED to let AJ go—after we got his contact information, of course.

He appeared to be clueless but not dangerous.

As soon as we climbed back into Michael's minivan, my phone rang. I looked at the screen. I didn't recognize the number but answered anyway.

"Elliot?" someone said.

"Who's speaking?" The voice sounded vaguely familiar, but I couldn't place it.

"This is Dennis from the Oleander Resort," the man said.

That's where I had heard that voice before. "Hi, Dennis. Is everything okay?"

I remembered those shears he'd had and reminded myself to be cautious.

"It was the strangest thing," Dennis started. "I was

talking to somebody else on the maintenance team today, and your father's name came up. My colleague started telling me that on the day your father died, he saw your father arguing with the resort manager, Palmer Birmingham."

"Is that right?" My pulse quickened at that news. I hadn't heard this before.

"I don't know if it's significant in any way, but I just thought you would want to know."

"I definitely want to know," I told him. "Thank you so much for sharing."

"Anything I can do to help," Dennis said. "Your father was a good man."

"Yes, he was."

I ended the call and glanced at Michael. I told him what Dennis just told me.

He glanced at his watch. "I have two hours left until I am supposed to pick up Chloe. Do you want to head back to the resort and see if Palmer Birmingham is there?"

"I would love to," I told him.

I didn't mind doing things by myself, but I always felt a surge of confidence when Michael was with me. There was so much I didn't know, and I still had instincts that I needed to refine.

We headed down the road to the Oleander Resort.

As we did, I imagined my dad driving this way to work every day. Was it hard for him to go from being a spy to a maintenance guy? I would imagine so. But he had been willing to make that sacrifice for our family.

At least, that was what I thought until yesterday.

What if he had come to this area and taken the job at Oleander for other reasons?

I had never thought of my dad as someone who harbored a lot of secrets. But now I was finding out that I was dead wrong. There was so much that I still needed to learn about my dad and his career and what was going on in his life in those days before he died.

No longer did I see his job as something that he had been made to do. I had a feeling he had chosen this job on purpose. And I wasn't sure how I felt about that.

Michael found a parking space, and we climbed out.

"You ready to do this?" Michael asked me.

"Ready as I'll ever be," I told him.

THE RECEPTIONIST DIDN'T WANT to let us talk to Palmer at first, but Michael was able to sweet-talk her until we were led back to his office. Maybe Michael and my dad were a lot more alike than I had thought. Just the way he'd charmed that woman made me think of my dad.

It was strange because I had never thought that about Michael before. But maybe he and my father did have more in common than I wanted to admit.

Palmer met us inside his office. Just as before, he looked all business as he turned toward us.

"Julie said this was urgent," he started. "What's going on?"

Michael nodded at me, indicating that I should go ahead.

I swallowed hard before saying, "As you know, my father worked here. It has come to my attention that on the day he died, the two of you argued."

A shadow crossed over his eyes, as if he hadn't expected to hear that. "Who told you?"

That wasn't exactly the response I had been expecting. "It's not important. Did you?"

He pressed his lips together before offering a curt nod. "Yes, we did. He thought I wasn't treating my employees fairly. I had to explain capitalism to him."

"What happened after that?" Michael asked.

Palmer sighed. "Nothing. I went to my office, and he went back to work. End of story."

"It sounds like you were pretty upset," Michael continued.

"I remained professional," Palmer said.

But I could hear a touch of anger creeping into his voice. Was he a hothead? Someone who could blow his top at a moment's notice?

I couldn't say for sure, but that was my best guess.

"Who found my father after his heart attack?"

"That would have been Dennis," Palmer said.

Had Dennis purposely implicated Palmer to throw me off his trail? Dennis would have had access to that room on the day of the lip-synching competition. Had his humble actions and soft-spoken voice fooled me?

I didn't know.

But somebody somewhere was not telling the truth.

"Is there anything else I can do for you? Because I have a meeting in," he looked at his watch, "three minutes."

"I think we're good," I told him. "Thank you for your help."

He nodded stiffly again before looking at the door. That was our cue to leave.

But I wasn't ready to get out of here yet.

I still had too much to figure out first.

CHAPTER TWENTY-EIGHT

A FEW MINUTES LATER, I headed toward one of those guest offices at the resort.

"Where are you going?" Michael asked, hurrying to keep step with me.

"I can't go back to the office now. And you have a little bit of time before you pick up Chloe, right?"

"Yes. But I still don't know where you're going."

"I'm trying to think all of this through," I told him, my thoughts speeding like an ocelot chasing a rabbit. "The only thing that makes sense is that it was somebody who works here at Oleander who killed Alejandro. Staff are the only ones who would have known where the security cameras were and how to cut them off and when. They could come and go easily without being noticed."

"So who do you think our suspects are?"

"I still haven't crossed Palmer off my list," I told him. "But what about Dennis?"

"He didn't give off the killer vibe," Michael said.

"He didn't. But that doesn't mean he's innocent."

"That's true. But you have no evidence to go on."

"He was the one who found my father. That should count for something. That fire starter that was shoved under the door? He probably had access to those. I know they have little firepits around here, especially in the cooler months."

"That could be true."

"And he's pointing the finger at all these different people. He directed us to the boat docks that day that we got shot at. Maybe after we left, he called someone and told him we were going over there."

"It is a possibility. More than one thing does seem connected to him."

"I don't want to believe that he did this. I mean, somebody who hated my father killed that man."

"What are you talking about?"

I realized what I said and clamped my mouth shut. That was right. I hadn't told him all of the details.

"I just mean . . ."

"Why don't you tell it to me straight, Elliot?" Michael leveled his gaze. "I know there's stuff you're keeping inside."

I looked away, trying to buy some time. It was no use. We didn't even have that much time right now.

"If I tell you something, you can't tell anybody else," I blurted. "Not even Oscar."

"What is it, Elliot?"

I swallowed. "You're not going to believe me."

"Try me."

I nodded before diving in. "My dad was a spy in Yerba. I believe that there are men here who wanted him dead. I believe one of those people may have killed my father and made it look like a heart attack."

"What?" Michael ran his hand through his hair. "You're serious?"

"I told you that you wouldn't believe me."

"It's not that I don't believe you," he said. "It's just . . . I never expected to hear that."

"I know how outlandish it sounds. I really do. But . . . it's true. It's a long story. It really is. But I now believe the man who was killed was trying to watch out for me. I learned he was a friend of my father's. I believe there was somebody else who did not want that man getting close to me."

"Why not?"

"I've asked myself that question too. The only thing I can figure is that maybe he wanted to tell me something. Tell me something that my father knew. Tell me something that someone desperately didn't want me to know."

"So someone intercepted him before he could talk to you and stabbed him?"

"That's the theory I'm playing with."

"So if this man was on your dad's side, then the man who killed him was on the side of the regime that took over in Yerba?"

"It's the only thing I can figure. But whoever these people are, they blend in. I probably couldn't pick them out of a crowd. That is what makes them good at what they do."

"Why would someone go through all this trouble? Killing your dad? Killing somebody who is going to talk to you? Next, are they going to try to kill you?"

I swallowed hard. So hard that my throat burned and I coughed.

Michael's words had been stark. But I needed to hear them. It was just that . . . hearing them out loud caused panic to surge.

"I did tell you that I thought someone had been following me. And someone tried to kill us more than once."

He let out another long breath, and then he looked at me as if searching for the right words. "Oh, Elliot . . ."

"I know," I said. "It's all crazy, right?"

"That's a true fact."

"So what are we going to do now?"

He glanced around. "Maybe the answers are all right here."

"Let's look at that video again." We slipped into an empty office beside us and closed the door. Nobody was in here so I hoped this worked in our favor. Then I pulled up that video on my phone, and we watched the footage of Alejandro slipping backstage.

Watching it now, armed with the information that he had been on my side, changed my entire perspective of it.

Had he slipped backstage hoping to catch me before I went on? What had he wanted to tell me? And how would someone have known he was going to be there in order to finish him off before he could?

I had so many questions I needed answers to.

I blinked, trying to get my gaze back into focus as the angle on my camera shifted. It swept down over Bruno's desk for a second before hovering back toward the screen.

"I feel like I'm missing something that's right there, but I can't pinpoint what," I told Michael.

"I've verified everybody on that screen. None of those people were guilty. I even stopped by the boutique one day after school and asked the employees there if they had seen anything while they were backstage. No one saw anything out of the ordinary."

"So where does this leave us?" I turned and leaned against the desk, facing Michael and hoping he had some insight he could share with me.

"Maybe it *is* someone who works here at the resort," Michael said. "It makes the most sense. They would know how to come and go the most easily."

"And Dennis told me that my father was arguing with three men a couple days before he died," I told Michael. "If my father's death really wasn't as natural as people said it was, then maybe his death does somehow revolve around this place."

"So who works here who might be guilty?" Michael asked.

"How about Palmer?"

"But if this somehow ties in with that jump drive, then he had every opportunity to grab it for himself without going through all this trouble."

"Good point," I said. "There's always Dennis. Maybe he's trying to throw us off by planting clues. And his gardening shears look like they might be the perfect murder weapon."

"I suppose that's something else that we could keep in mind."

Before we could talk anymore, I heard the door click behind us. I twirled around, anticipating the worst.

But the person I saw there made my mouth drop open.

CHAPTER TWENTY-NINE

"HEADSET MAN," I muttered.

The man who had been in charge of directing the lip-synching competition stood there, a crazy look in his eyes as he shut the door behind him.

Michael wedged himself in front of me as the man stepped closer.

"You two ruined my competition," he muttered. "Now nobody even wants to reschedule."

The man's pupils were dilated, and his words were overly pronounced. Spittle flew from his mouth.

He was definitely upset.

"It's not our fault the competition was ruined," I told him. "You can blame it on whoever murdered that man."

"This is my crowning achievement here at the resort,"

Headset Man said. "Out of everything I do, this is my favorite. And, now, its reputation has been tarnished."

"What exactly do you do here at the resort?" I did remember that he had been backstage. He would have been privy to anything going on. And that day after Michael and I had been trapped in the room with the smoke, I had seen him watching us.

So who was this guy really?

"I'm the director of special events," Headset Man said. "I usually have to do stupid golf tournaments or regattas. I hate it. But the lip-synching competition? Now that is what true entertainment is all about."

"So why did you kill that man?" Michael said.

Headset Man froze, all the color drained from his face. "Me? Why in the world would I kill him?"

"Isn't that why you came in here?" I asked. "Because you killed him and now you want to kill us too?"

The man took a step back. "I would never kill somebody. I just know that the two of you keep stirring up trouble, so when I saw you slip in here, I decided this would be a great opportunity to give you two a piece of my mind."

"So you didn't kill that man?" Michael confirmed.

"Of course, I didn't kill anybody. What kind of a man do you think I am?" The way he pulled his face back, causing his chin to disappear, made it clear he was appalled at the idea.

"Did you see anything while you were backstage?" I

asked. "Because if we can figure out what happened, then maybe your competition can be saved."

I couldn't believe the words had just left my lips. The last thing I wanted was for this competition to be rescheduled. I wanted out of it.

"I didn't see anything backstage. I was too busy trying to gather all the contestants and make sure they got onstage in time."

"You'd never before seen the man who died?" I asked.

"I had not."

"And you don't know of anyone here at the resort who might have killed him then?" Michael said.

"Like I told you," the man said, "everybody has their nose up in the air, and they think they're better than other people. But does that mean they would actually kill somebody? If you ask me, jail would not be the accommodations these hoity-toities were looking for."

I couldn't argue with that point. "Thanks for your help."

Headset Man leaned closer and lowered his voice. "Find this killer. And save my competition. Please."

I wished I could promise him that we could do that.

But it was feeling less certain all the time.

I TURNED to Michael once Headset Man left. "That was unexpected."

He sagged against the table. "Yeah, tell me about it."

"There's gotta be something here that we're missing," I told Michael. "I feel like we are so close."

"Let's say it was someone here who killed him. And let's say we can rule out the headset man. That still leaves us with Palmer. And possibly Dennis."

"Blaine told me something when I talked to him today," I told Michael.

"Who's Blaine?"

I shook my head, realizing I had too many thoughts shoved inside. "Sorry. He was an ambassador to Yerba. I met with him this morning. Anyway, he said it was someone who blended in. That it wouldn't be someone who looked like you might expect."

"There was the assistant manager who left suddenly," Michael said. "We haven't looked into him."

"And there is the fact that Mr. Harrington owns this place also. We can't forget about that either."

"Let's talk about the murder weapon," Michael said. "It was something short and thick. Besides the gardening shears, what else might it be?"

"I don't know enough about weapons to be able to tell you. I just assumed a knife was a knife."

"It would have to be something smaller, otherwise it would have been too obvious to the people around us."

I mentally replayed that video image.

And I sat up straight.

"I think I might know who did it," I muttered. "The answer was right in front of me the whole time, I just didn't see it."

"Who?" Michael asked.

I was still busy kicking myself. Why did it take me this long to see it? I was supposed to be the detail person.

But that didn't matter right now. What mattered was the fact that I might actually have a suspect.

Before I could voice my thoughts aloud, my phone rang. I glanced at the screen and saw it was my mom.

I was halfway surprised she was still speaking with me after our last conversation.

After a moment of hesitation, I put the phone to my ear. "Mama?"

"Elliot, someone broke into our house."

CHAPTER THIRTY

"WHAT? WHAT HAPPENED? ARE YOU OKAY?" The questions rushed from my lips.

Michael appeared beside me, leaning in close so he could hear.

"I'm fine," Mom said. "I just got home, and everything was torn apart."

"Is anything missing?" I asked.

"It's hard to tell. Of course, there's not much here that has any value."

My mind raced. I thought about that jewelry box. I thought about the journal my father had left there.

Had this person who'd broken in taken that?

My heart pounded in my ears at the thought. Maybe I should have made copies of it. Maybe I should have hidden it somewhere a little more clever.

And what about the jump drive? Had someone been looking for that? It was my best guess.

I was so thankful that no one had been home when this person had broken in.

"Did you call the police?" I asked.

"I just did," my mom said. "They're on their way so they can take a report."

"I'll be home as soon as I can so I can help you sort through everything and clean up, okay?"

"Of course," my mom said. "At times like this, I really just miss your father . . ."

"I know, Mama." My voice broke. "We all do."

I ended the call and looked up at Michael. This wasn't good.

"You think this has something to do with what's going on?" He stared at me, waiting for my response.

"It's the only thing that makes sense. These people are coming after my family now. I have to do something about it."

"I'm sorry this is happening to you, Elliot." He stepped closer and rubbed my arm.

The sincere concern in his eyes made my heart thump double-time for a minute.

I was so glad that God sent him into my life. He had always been there for me. And someone like that was exactly whom I had been praying for.

"I need to talk something through with you," I started.

"And then I need to get home and check on my mom. But I cannot leave here without knowing if I'm right."

Michael sat down in a chair and waited for me to continue.

IT TOOK me a moment to compose my thoughts. I knew I might sound crazy.

But what if I didn't?

I pulled out my phone and found that video footage that I had taken of the moments before Alejandro had died.

"Look at this," I started.

Michael leaned closer, close enough that I could smell his spicy cologne. "What am I looking at?"

"Not at the obvious," I said, shaking my head. "That's why I can't believe I've missed it all this time."

"I'm still not following what you're saying, Elliot."

"What I'm saying is this. Whoever is behind this was able to access this video feed. He was able to delete the critical moments in the video that the police would have seen in order to apprehend the killer. He would have had eyes on everything that's happening here. And he had the know-how to be able to kill Alejandro without anyone noticing."

"Exactly," Michael said. "But who do you think it is?"

I pointed to the video screen. But not at the video itself.

Instead, I fast forwarded to the moment my camera had

dipped lower and swept over the desk where the video controller was located.

There was a photo there. A photo of a man in military uniform.

"I don't know much about the US military. But I do know a few things. Look at the hat in this photo."

Michael blew the image up and squinted as he stared at it. "Those are the kinds that Green Berets wear, right?"

"Exactly. And what are Green Berets known for?"

"For special forces. They know how to kill someone and get away with it . . ." Michael's voice trailed.

"We've been talking to a killer this whole time, and we haven't realized it," I told him.

"We need to call Hunter," Michael said. "Because I think you're right. The killer is right here at the resort."

"I knew you would figure it out sooner or later," someone said behind us.

When I turned this time, I knew it was the real killer I was looking at.

CHAPTER THIRTY-ONE

"BRUNO . . ." I muttered.

But I wasn't even looking at his face.

No, I stared at the gun he held in his hands.

A gun that was pointed directly at me.

"You should have left it alone," Bruno said. "It's a good thing I learned to read lips."

"Why is that?" I asked, wondering what in the world that had to do with anything.

A sly smile crossed his face. "Because when I'm watching the camera feeds, I can understand exactly what people are saying. I knew you were going to figure out that it was me. It was just a matter of time."

"We should have seen it sooner." Michael shook his head, almost looking disappointed with himself. "You were the most obvious person who could take down those cameras when you did."

"Exactly. I was the one who knew how to do it. You should have stayed out of it."

"I still don't understand," I muttered. "Why would you kill Alejandro? Why was he a threat to you?"

"Because he was trying to get to you," Bruno said. "There are people who want the new regime in Yerba to fail, and they'll do anything they can to make that happen."

"What does that have to do with me?" My voice rose in pitch. He wasn't making sense.

"Your father knew things that could bring us down, destroy us. We had to stop him."

"And Alejandro . . ."

"He wouldn't give up. He wanted to talk to you. To pull you into this."

I shook my head, trying to comprehend that. "Why?"

"You don't know?"

"Know what?" I was beginning to feel stupid right about now.

"Your dad had information on us, information that we want."

"Where is it?" I knew it was a long shot that he would share any of that information. But the words had escaped before I could stop them.

"You tell me," he growled.

The jump drive practically burned a hole in my jeans.

"How did you get involved with the new regime in Yerba?" I asked, trying to put all the pieces together.

Bruno's gaze clouded. "I went down there after I got out of the military. Met a girl, and we shacked up together for a while. One thing led to another, and I met up with the right people—people who wanted to build a better government. I knew I wanted to do what I could to help. But the men in charge had jobs for me to do here in the States."

"How many of you are there?" Michael asked.

"That's not something that I'm going to share with you. Just know, Elliot, that your father was the number one person on our radar."

"Is that why you killed him?"

Bruno tilted his head. "I didn't kill your father. He would have been better off to me alive."

I gripped my hands, my fingernails digging into my palms as I clenched them. "Then why couldn't you just have left him alone?"

"It doesn't matter anymore," Bruno said. "Now I'm going to need to take care of the two of you. Lucky for me, the cameras are down again. Maybe we can have the two of you try to steal another boat."

"You know we didn't try to steal that boat," Michael muttered.

"No, you didn't. But that's what I can make this look like."

"Did you chase me down that day on my way home? And try to run Michael and me over outside The Burger Joint? Was that all you?"

"There's more than one person at play here," Bruno said. "Whoever gets to you first will be rewarded. I could use some extra cash."

My throat tightened at the thought. How many people were there, exactly, trying to kill me?

"We're going to walk outside, and neither of you are going to make a move," Bruno continued. "It's going to look like the three of us are just friends walking and talking today. Got it?"

"You don't want to do this," Michael said.

"That's where you're wrong. I really do want to do this."

I couldn't let that happen. I could not let Michael get hurt because of me. I reached into my pocket and felt the ribbon that Chloe had handed me earlier. The one I'd offered to get the knots out of.

It was the only weapon at my disposal right now. But what could I do with it?

Bruno motioned for Michael to go out the door.

Michael exchanged a glance with me before taking a step toward the hallway.

Bruno slipped his gun into his coat pocket to conceal it, even though I knew it was still pointed at Michael.

I had to make a snap decision.

Before I could second-guess myself, I hopped on Bruno's back and pulled out the ribbon. I wrapped it around his neck.

The action was abrupt enough that it threw Bruno off. He struggled against the string around his neck, his hand leaving his gun for a moment.

That gave Michael enough time to reach into the man's pocket and grab it. Just as Bruno slammed me into the wall behind us, Michael aimed the gun at him.

"Freeze!"

Bruno did just as he said. As he did, I slid off him and backed away, trying to slow my racing heart. That may not have been my wisest move, but at least it had worked.

For now.

"Call the police," Michael directed.

Bruno raised his hands. "You don't want to do that. I can explain."

"We don't want to hear any more of your explanations," Michael said. "We just want you behind bars. Where you belong."

I pulled out my phone and dialed Hunter's number. He promised he would be here soon.

In the meantime, Michael handed me the gun and then took that ribbon and tied Bruno's hands behind his back.

"How did you know it was me?" Bruno asked.

"When I took that cell phone video, I accidentally

captured one of the pictures on your desk. It showed you when you were in the military. You were a Green Beret, right?"

"I was until that explosion took me out of service." His eyes narrowed with irritation.

"Green Berets are known for their special forces knives and clandestine skills. It suddenly made sense to me that you were the most logical person to kill Alejandro. You're short enough that you could have walked backstage among the contestants and people might not have noticed you. And you would have known exactly where to stab Alejandro so he would die instantly. That's what you needed."

"You have a lot of enemies out there, Elliot." Bruno's gaze narrowed. "You should've just let me be the one to take you in."

"What do you want me for?" I asked.

Bruno struggled against his binds, but Michael stood behind him, holding them in place.

"Your dad had something that we want."

My throat tightened as I remembered that jump drive. "What's that?"

"I think you know the answer to that question."

"Maybe I do," I finally said. "What kind of information exactly is it that has someone feeling so threatened?"

"There's a lot you don't know about what went on in Yerba. It's probably better if you don't know. You should just hand over the information and be done with it. Before anyone else gets hurt."

"Who else could get hurt?" I almost didn't want to know the answer to that question.

"These people will do anything to get the answers they want. Believe me. I'm not the only one out there."

Michael pulled him closer and growled into his ear, "Who are you working for?"

"It's not important." Bruno smiled, but as he did his eyelids began to droop. "If you hadn't interfered with things . . ."

Something wasn't right, I realized. What was going on?

"Who were the men who met with my father a couple days before he died?" I rushed.

Bruno's eyes drooped again. "Like I said, I'm not the only one out there . . ."

Bruno's entire body seemed to go limp. He sank to the floor, and foam began coming out of his mouth.

"What's going on?" I asked Michael. I still didn't take the gun off him just in case this was some type of scheme.

Michael turned him over onto his side while his mouth continued to foam and his body convulsed.

"I think he took a pill. Something that would ensure nobody would be getting any answers from him anytime soon."

"But his hands were bound . . ."

"He probably had it in his mouth as a precaution."

Just as he said the words, the police rushed into the room and took over the scene.

But I hoped this wasn't the final answer from Bruno. Because I had other questions that I desperately needed answers to.

CHAPTER THIRTY-TWO

HUNTER TURNED toward me after I had given him my statement about what had happened. "I'm glad you're okay, Elliot."

I pulled my arms over my chest even tighter as I nodded. "Me too. It was touch and go there for a while."

"Doesn't look like we're going to be getting any information out of Bruno," Hunter said. "You know that the paramedics weren't able to revive him."

Disappointment pressed on me. But his news hadn't been a surprise to me. I had ascertained those facts as I stood in the background watching. "I know. But that's too bad."

"It really is. I know you just want to put an end to all of this."

"I do. But at least we know who killed Alejandro. Still, it

doesn't comfort me knowing that there are more men out there who are just like him."

"Now that we know a little bit about what's going on, we'll be able to keep our eyes open more. We will pore through Bruno's records and see if we can find any indications of who he might have been working for."

I shivered again. That was right. He was working for someone. Most likely, someone powerful. Someone who was paying him to do the dirty work. And someone who had a connection with the new Yerba government.

"Thank you again for your help," I told him.

My throat felt dry as I looked up at him. In an instant, I remembered our kiss. About how sweet and tender and perfect it had felt . . . until he had apologized for it.

"Look, Elliot . . ." He leaned closer. "About the other night."

"Never mind," I said. "You don't have to say anything."

"But I do. I know I bungled it." He stared off in the distance for a moment. "The kiss was great. I'm just not sure I'm ready to jump into something yet."

"I feel the same way. It's not a big deal."

"Maybe we could just keep getting to know each other for a while."

My lips pulled up in a smile. "I would like that."

Hunter smiled also. "Good. I'm glad you're on board also."

In the distance, one of his officers called him over.

"I'll talk to you later," Hunter said.

I nodded. "I look forward to it."

I watched him walk back over to the scene. As he did, Michael came from around the hallway and met me. "Are you okay?"

"You gotta stop asking me that," I said.

"You've got to stop getting yourself in trouble then."

"You're my teacher," I told him.

"I'm not sure anybody would ever be able to teach you how to stay away from trouble. You seem to be a magnet for it."

"Well, if that isn't the sweetest thing anyone's ever said."

"Very funny." His expression turned serious. "I really do worry about you, Elliot. Especially after everything we learned today."

"I'm not going to lie. I'm a little worried too. Not just about me. But about my mom and my sister."

His jaw tightened. "I know. I don't like the sound of this. We have to figure out who the ringleader is behind all of this."

"Whoever it is, he must be powerful."

Michael glanced around. "Do you know if you can leave yet?"

"No one said I had to stay. And you've got to pick up Chloe . . . how could I have forgotten?"

"Don't worry. I called her friend's mom, and she said it

was okay if she stayed for a little bit longer. I thought you might be ready to get home now."

"I am." My mom and I needed to talk.

One thing was certain, however.

I dreaded seeing the disappointment in her gaze.

I STEPPED into my house and paused. The couch cushions were strewn all over the room, the coffee table was overturned, books from the shelves on either side of the TV now littered the floor.

My throat tightened.

Someone had clearly been looking for something.

But then, in the middle of the destruction, I spotted my mom. She sat at the kitchen table, her Bible open in front of her and a cup of tea beside it. She barely glanced at me as I walked inside.

That was never a good sign.

"Hello, Mama." I put my purse down and paced over toward her.

"Hello, Elliot."

I could tell by the stiffness in her voice that she still wasn't happy with me.

"It's a mess in here," I murmured.

"We'll get it cleaned up. First, I just needed to take a few minutes to get my thoughts focused."

"I'm glad you're okay." My throat burned. I meant the words. I was so glad my mom hadn't been home when this happened.

"Me too. All of this . . . it's just stuff. Stuff can be replaced. People cannot."

I sat down across from her quietly. "Where's Ruth?"

"She went to the beach with her friends earlier today. I dropped her off myself."

As an awkward silence fell between us, I realized that this was going to be even harder than I thought. I knew that what was going on in my heart was more important than the destruction in this house. No doubt that was what my mom thought as well.

"Look, Mama," I finally started. "I just want to say I'm sorry—"

Her gaze shot up to meet mine. "How could you be working for a private investigator? That line of work isn't safe. I've already lost your father. Do you want me to lose you too?"

Her words made my throat tighten. I knew exactly what kind of pain she was experiencing. I hated for her to go through any of this.

"Of course, I don't want you to lose me too," I said. "But I actually feel like I'm doing something that I'm good at. That I'm making a difference."

"But you're so good at networking as an administrator. Why don't you do something like that again? Something behind the scenes."

"My whole life I thought that that's what I should do. That I wasn't meant to be out in front. There's a part of me that still doesn't like it. But there's another part of me that just wants to give it a shot. We've only got one chance to do this life. I don't want to hide behind my fears."

"Oh, Elliot . . ." My mom frowned. "You sound so much like your father."

"He was a 'take the bull by the horns' kind of guy, wasn't he?"

"Yes, he was. I have to say, if he were still alive, he would probably tell me that I should let you keep this job."

"You think?"

"He always told me I should give you more freedom," Mama said. "And I always pushed back. I've always wanted to protect you."

"Maybe it's my chance now to protect you."

She reached across the table and squeezed my hand. "I can't let you get hurt."

"I don't want to get hurt."

She stared at me for a moment and said nothing. But I could see in her eyes that she was beginning to accept this new job that I'd taken. I could be grateful for that at least.

I cleared my throat. "Mama, I know this seems off topic, but . . . did anyone from the Oleander Resort ever call and tell you about some items that dad had left in his locker there?"

I halfway expected to see surprise register across her face, but I didn't. She knew exactly what I was talking about.

She glanced into her tea before rubbing her throat. "They did. I couldn't bring myself to go and pick them up, though. I knew it was probably just some spare clothes, maybe some sunscreen or some lip balm. I just didn't think I could handle it."

"But you seem to handle everything so well."

"I try to. I try to hold it together on the outside. But on the inside? I feel like I'm dying too." Her voice trembled with emotion.

I squeezed her hand. "I'm so sorry, Mama. I can't imagine what you are going through."

"I miss him so much, Elliot."

"I miss him so much too." I licked my lips and contemplated my next question. "I never did ask—exactly why did we come to Storm River? Why here of all places, instead of going to Georgia where you still have some family?"

"Your dad said that the best hospitals for your sister's condition were located in the DC area. But DC was too expensive to live in. Then he found this job at the Oleander Resort and so we came here." She studied my face. "Why are you asking?"

"I was just curious. I guess when I was at the Oleander for the lip-synching competition, some questions popped up in my head."

She continued to study me. "Is that all?"

I wanted to ask her if she knew about my dad's secret career. The question was on the tip of my tongue.

But if she didn't know, then I didn't think that now was the time to break the news to her. Instead, I decided to save that secret for another day. "The resort manager gave me a bag of Papa's things. You're right. It was just some extra clothes and some small things. I'll bring them inside later."

"Thanks. By the way, I did get a little bit of good news today." My mom's countenance seemed to lift. "Ruth is now number nineteen on the transplant list."

I sucked in a breath. "That *is* great news, Mama. Really great."

"At this rate, it could be any day. Or it could still be months. We just don't know."

I hated to be the one to bring up the cold hard facts of reality in the middle of such good news, but . . . "How are we moneywise?"

Some of the light left her gaze. "We still need about fifty thousand dollars to pay for the surgery. I need to sign something before she goes in promising that I have the money."

How were we going to get all that money before her surgery? I got paid about seven hundred a week. Even if I saved all my wages just for the surgery, it would still take me more than a year to have enough.

My heart felt heavy at the thought of it. "Maybe I should get a second job in the evenings."

"The Lord will provide," my mom said. "He always does,

and we need to trust that He's going to do the same in this situation right now."

Her words reminded me that I needed to have faith. But sometimes that was easier said than done.

Finally, I nodded. "You're right. I should try not to worry about it so much."

As my mom's phone buzzed, she looked down at the screen and let out a sigh. "I'm going to work an extra shift tonight at the drugstore. It's time for me to get ready. I can clean this up later."

"I'll help. Don't worry about it." She had enough things on her mind. "It was good talking to you, Mama."

She stood and squeezed my hand. "You too, Elliot. We'll talk again later, okay?"

I nodded. "Okay."

CHAPTER THIRTY-THREE

AS MY MOM got ready for work, I slipped into my room.

I could hardly breathe as I walked toward my nightstand.

My room had also been torn apart, similar to the rest of the house. My bedspread was on the floor. Clothes were all over the place. Pictures that had been on the wall were now smashed and out of sight.

But there was only one thing I could think about.

I paused by my bed.

The jewelry box my father had made me.

Where was it?

My heart lodged into my throat as I moved some clothes aside, desperately looking for it. What if the people who'd broken in had taken it? What if they had my dad's journal?

I could hardly bear the thought of it.

I moved the clothes but didn't see it.

My throat seemed to clog even more, almost until I couldn't breathe.

Where was it?

I swung my head around, searching for the wooden box.

I didn't see it anywhere.

No, no, no!

Finally, I got on my hands and knees. I looked under my bed.

It wasn't there.

Looked under more clothes.

Not there either.

I crawled to my closet.

After moving more clothing, my breath caught.

Could it be . . . ?

I reached forward and my hands felt the smooth wood.

It was!

The jewelry box!

Quickly, I hit the false edge at the bottom—where the journal was kept.

The drawer popped out and there inside . . . was the journal!

My heart cried out with joy.

I grabbed the leather-bound book and held it to my chest as tears rushed to my eyes.

Thank goodness, they hadn't found it.

A FEW MINUTES LATER, Michael picked me up. He said hello to my mom as she was leaving for work and promised her that he was still interested in coming to eat with us sometime. My mom looked delighted.

Then Michael and I took off. As soon as I got back home, I would straighten the house. But there were a few other things I needed to take care of first.

His parents had arrived back from their various destinations and were spending some time with Chloe.

That gave us a little bit of time to take care of some much-needed business.

Business concerning my father's jump drive.

Michael had called his friend who was good at accessing encoded information, and we were going to meet at this guy's apartment.

"No one's supposed to know this, but he works for the CIA," Michael told me.

My heart thumped in my chest. The CIA?

I never thought I'd somehow find myself mixed up in this clandestine world. But here I was.

"You're sure we can trust this guy?" I asked.

"I'm sure. We went to college together. I would trust him with my life."

I felt if Michael said that, that I could trust this guy too. But that didn't stop my nerves from capturing my muscles and causing a slight shiver there. I didn't know what I was going to find on the jump drive, and part of me didn't want to know. But I knew I couldn't rest until I did everything within my power to figure out what exactly my father had been killed for.

"Elliot," Michael started. "I don't want to sound like your father, but I don't like how any of this sounds. If what Bruno said is correct, then there's a whole group of people out there with ties to Yerba. They think that you have something that could bring down this new regime. It sounds dangerous. And the fact that we don't know who the rest of these guys are? Or what they look like? It leaves me with a really bad feeling in my gut."

"Me too," I told him. I wished I could deny it. But I would be a fool if that was the case.

All my fears were coming to fruition. Now my family was in danger. Michael knew what was going on also. Did that mean that he and Chloe might also be in danger?

I had no idea.

We pulled up to an apartment building on the outskirts of DC. I felt sick to my stomach as Michael and I entered the building and climbed two sets of stairs.

A moment later, he knocked on the door, and a man around our age answered.

"Elliot, this is Grayson," Michael said. "Grayson, Elliot."

We nodded at each other stiffly, almost as if we both knew the implications of this meeting.

Grayson ushered us inside before glancing up and down the hallway. "Did anyone follow you?"

"No, I kept my eye on the road the whole time and even took a few extra twists and turns just to make sure," Michael said. "We should be safe."

Grayson led us into a dark bedroom that he had set up as an office. He probably had six computer screens there.

"Now, what's this about a jump drive?" he started.

As always, I could feel the device burning through my jeans. It was in my pocket again, as close to me as I could possibly get it.

"My father left it, and you need a code to get into it," I started. "I'm afraid if I try too many times and fail that I'll never be able to get in. Can you help?"

"There are ways to get around these things," Grayson said, pushing up his glasses. "But it's going to take some time."

"I know," I told him, feeling the sweat start to spread across my hands. "I'm going to need you to use your discretion here."

"Of course. If my superiors knew that I was doing this, I could get in trouble also. So it goes both ways."

Knowing that actually made me feel a little better.

He extended his hand. And I knew he was waiting for that jump drive.

After a moment of hesitation, I pulled it from my pocket and placed it in his palm. "Here you go."

"Let's see what you've got," Grayson said. He sat down at his desk.

"I'll go get some water for us," Michael offered.

"That sounds great," Grayson said. "This will probably take a while."

As Michael disappeared from the room, I pulled up the next chair and sat beside Grayson. My throat felt tight as I waited to see what would happen next.

"So you're a friend of Michael's, huh?" Grayson started.

"That's right. We work together."

"Michael's a good guy," Grayson said. "He doesn't let very many people get close to him."

"I've noticed."

"Once he gives someone his loyalty, then that person has his loyalty for always. And that can be a good or a bad thing."

I didn't know what Grayson was getting at, but I continued to listen.

"I see," I said.

"For years, he was loyal to Chloe's mom, even after everything she put him through," Grayson said. "I thought he would never get over her."

My heart thumped in my ears. I'd never heard that side of the story before, but I'd always wondered about it.

"I'm just saying, if he lets you in, you should feel honored."

"I know. I will," I said.

Now I was even more curious than ever about Michael and his past.

Before I could ask any more questions, Michael appeared with three bottles of water and took a seat next to us.

Grayson inserted the jump drive into his computer and waited.

The seconds seemed to drag by at an agonizingly slow pace.

What was taking so long?

Finally, Grayson let out a grunt and began tapping at his keyboard. "This is going to be harder than I thought."

"What do you mean?" I asked.

"This jump drive has some pretty high tech encoding on it. This wasn't done by some wannabe hacker."

"I see." I supposed that made sense. My dad had been a spy. He wasn't going to have classified information accessible for just anybody.

Grayson typed several more things into his computer before letting out another grunt and turning to us. "I'm not going to be able to get through this today. I'm going to need a couple days probably. The last thing I want to do is to make a wrong move and end up having everything on this jump drive erased."

I sucked in a breath. "That can happen?"

"Unfortunately, yes. But I'm careful. I just need time so I can figure it out."

"You okay with that, Elliot?" Michael asked.

I thought about it for a moment. I desperately didn't want

to leave this jump drive behind. I didn't have any other choice here. I didn't know whom else I could trust.

Finally, I nodded. "Okay. If that's what we need to do."

"I'll get in touch with you guys as soon as I know something," Grayson said. "And be careful on your way out. I don't want anyone to know that you were here."

I didn't like the sound of that. All of this cloak and dagger stuff was a little bit too much for me. But I'd been thrown into a real-life spy scenario.

As Michael and I left, he slipped an arm around my shoulder and pulled me into a quick hug.

"It's going to be okay, Elliot."

There he went again, spouting his familiar phrases. But I had to admit that there was part of me that really appreciated them.

"Thanks for going above and beyond to help me," I told him.

"That's what friends are for."

A smile stretched across my lips. Friends. I was so grateful to have at least one in my life right now.

CHAPTER THIRTY-FOUR

A WEEK LATER, I stood backstage at the Oleander Resort. My lungs felt tight, and I'd come up with so many rhymes that my head was spinning. None of them had made sense.

Michael walked up behind me and rubbed my shoulders. "It's going to be fine."

He had to tell me those familiar words all the time.

Even though a week had passed, Grayson still hadn't been able to crack the code and access that jump drive. He wasn't giving up yet.

But that meant I still didn't have any answers.

The good news was that there hadn't been any more attempts on my life. Maybe it had something to do with the fact that Hunter had a car patrolling my house every thirty minutes or so.

He hadn't told me that. But I'd seen the cop cars. I knew what was going on.

And I appreciated it. For my mom's and sister's sakes more than for my own. The more people who could watch out for them, the better.

"I thought that if I somehow solved this case, that that would absolve me from having to do this," I muttered.

"You guys have just made me the happiest man alive," a new voice said.

I looked over and saw Headset Man appear.

I narrowed my eyes. "We didn't do this for you."

"Doesn't matter to me why you did it. The only thing that matters is that we get to complete this lip-synching competition."

"Yay," I said with fake enthusiasm.

Before we could talk anymore, I heard the emcee on stage announce that it was our turn.

Oscar turned to us. "Are we ready to win this? I know we have what it takes to beat that burger joint this year."

I wished I felt as confident. I could barely remember any of my moves. And what if I somehow didn't line myself up right and we were off balance? I would never live it down if Ms. Symmetry hadn't been symmetrical.

I didn't have any more time to think about it. I was ushered onstage, and I took my place behind Oscar.

The audience cheered. I made the mistake of looking out at them for a minute. I saw my mom and Ruth there.

My gaze scanned the crowd until it stopped on Hunter.

We had talked on the phone a few times, and he had told me that he would like to come and see us perform.

I didn't tell anybody who was here to support me that I would rather they weren't here to see my humiliation.

That would have been rude so I'd kept those thoughts to myself.

Now I was wishing that I hadn't been so polite.

I also spotted Jono out there. A woman I'd never seen before sat beside him.

Mr. Harrington was there.

So were Chloe and her grandparents.

The music started. I got myself in position, head lowered with only my cowboy hat showing.

And then we began our routine. It had a little bit of line dancing and a whole lot of acting and a whole lot of lip moving.

Michael and I acted out the roles we had been assigned. He put an arm around Velma, acting like he was taking a picture of them, and then I walked onto the scene and gave Michael a shove.

That was right. Private Eyes at work, causing all those achy breaky hearts to be known.

Surprisingly, once I got started, I felt like I remembered most of what I was supposed to do. I could be thankful for that.

As the song ended, we took our spots for the closing

pose. Then the lights onstage went down, and the audience burst into applause.

It seemed like they really liked us.

The emcee walked onstage and dismissed us as we slipped offstage.

I was *so* glad to have that over with.

"See," Michael said. "I told you that wasn't going to be terrible. You did a great job."

"You all did a great job," Oscar said. "I'm going to treat you all to dinner after that . . . provided that we win, of course. And that there are no murders between now and the end."

Michael and I both moaned. Did he have any idea how close to reality his words hit?

Thirty minutes later, all the contestants waited onstage to hear who'd won.

"Our top three are . . ." The emcee looked at his paper. "The Burger Joint, Madison's Motors, and . . . Driscoll and Associates."

My heart skipped a beat.

We'd come this far. That was a good sign, right?

All three teams stepped forward.

"Coming in second place is . . . The Burger Joint!"

The audience applauded.

That meant that we'd either gotten third or first. I held my breath as I waited to see.

"And this year's champion is . . ."

Oscar's chest puffed out beside us. He was fully expecting our name to be called.

"'All the Single Ladies' with Madison's Motors!"

More applause came from the audience.

But Oscar's face remained placid as he tried to hide his disappointment.

"It was a good try," Velma said. "At least there's going to be cake afterward."

She was probably already planning to take some home.

"Next year," Oscar whispered. "Next year, we're winning this."

I held back a groan.

I was going to have to keep doing things outside my comfort zone, wasn't I?

But maybe those things were good for me. They pushed me to a place where I would grow.

And I was going to need all the growth I could muster if I was going to find out answers about my father's death.

COMING NEXT: THE PRACTICE OF
PRYING

#7 Mucky Streak

#8 Foul Play

#9 Broom & Gloom

#10 Dust and Obey

#11 Thrill Squeaker

#11.5 Swept Away (novella)

#12 Cunning Attractions

#13 Cold Case: Clean Getaway

#14 Cold Case: Clean Sweep

#15 Cold Case: Clean Break

While You Were Sweeping, A Riley Thomas Spinoff

THE WORST DETECTIVE EVER:

I'm not really a private detective. I just play one on TV.

Joey Darling, better known to the world as Raven Remington, detective extraordinaire, is trying to separate herself from her invincible alter ego. She played the spunky character for five years on the hit TV show *Relentless*, which catapulted her to fame and into the role of Hollywood's sweetheart. When her marriage falls apart, her finances dwindle to nothing, and her father disappears, Joey finds herself on the Outer Banks of North Carolina, trying to piece together her life away from the limelight. But as people continually mistake her for the character she played on TV, she's tasked with solving real life crimes . . . even though she's terrible at it.

#1 Ready to Fumble

#2 Reign of Error

#3 Safety in Blunders

#4 Join the Flub

#5 Blooper Freak

#6 Flaw Abiding Citizen

#7 Gaffe Out Loud

#8 Joke and Dagger

#9 Wreck the Halls

#10 Glitch and Famous (coming soon)

ABOUT THE AUTHOR

USA Today has called Christy Barritt's books "scary, funny, passionate, and quirky."

Christy writes both mystery and romantic suspense novels that are clean with underlying messages of faith. Her books have won the Daphne du Maurier Award for Excellence in Suspense and Mystery, have been twice nominated for the Romantic Times Reviewers' Choice Award, and have finaled for both a Carol Award and Foreword Magazine's Book of the Year.

She is married to her Prince Charming, a man who thinks she's hilarious—but only when she's not trying to be. Christy is a self-proclaimed klutz, an avid music lover who's known for spontaneously bursting into song, and a road trip aficionado.

When she's not working or spending time with her family, she enjoys singing, playing the guitar, and exploring small, unsuspecting towns where people have no idea how accident-prone she is.

Find Christy online at:

www.christybarritt.com
www.facebook.com/christybarritt
www.twitter.com/cbarritt

Sign up for Christy's newsletter to get information on all of her latest releases here: **www.christybarritt.com/newsletter-sign-up/**

If you enjoyed this book, please consider leaving a review.